D1099014

READING
OREGON
TRAIL

CHILDREN
ON THE
OREGON
TRAIL

A. RUTGERS VAN DER LOEFF

Hodder
Children's
Books

a division of Hodder Headline

First published as *De Kinderkaravaan* in Holland in 1954

This translation and adaptation entitled *Children on the Oregon Trail* copyright © 1961 Oxford University Press

Published in paperback in 1963 by Puffin Books, a division of Penguin Books Ltd, 27 Wrights Lane, London W8 5TZ

This paperback edition published in Great Britain in 2000 by Hodder Children's Books

10 9 8 7 6 5 4 3 2 1

A Catalogue record for this book is available from the British Library

ISBN 0 340 77325 1

Typeset by Avon Dataset Ltd, Bidford-on-Avon, Warks

Printed and bound in Great Britain by The Guernsey Press Co. Ltd, Channel Isles

Hodder Children's Books
A Division of Hodder Headline
338 Euston Road
London NW1 3BH

Introduction

A friend of mine once sent me a Swiss newspaper in which a short article had been enthusiastically ringed in red. It contained a brief account of the historic journey made by the seven Sager children through the north-west of America in 1844, in the days when the West was still a desolate wilderness full of perils.

The subject so fascinated me that I started to investigate. Books on the history of American pioneering, old diaries of emigrants who had gone to the Far West at that same time cast, now and again, a ray of light on this unimaginable children's adventure. In addition, an old letter on the subject, written by the factor of a small fur-trading post, had been preserved, and a report by the well-known American medical missionary Marcus Whitman, who worked among the Indians in the Columbia valley.

It is on these plain historical facts that the present story has been based.

It all happened more than a hundred years ago. In those days North America was, for the most part, an unknown, undeveloped country. Up till then only explorers and fur trappers had wandered through the immense forests, over the rolling prairies, and across the rugged mountains. Now it was the turn of the first pioneers – men and women with children, who looked for a new life in a new land. It was the time when the Americans in the east swarmed out into the undeveloped West, in order to take possession of millions and millions of acres of new ground.

When John Sager was eight years old, his father also caught the pioneering fever. The family loaded all their goods and chattels into a covered wagon, harnessed four oxen to it, and left the east coast of the United States for the Middle West.

That long journey, over the mountains, along the valleys, and through the deep forests of half America, was a tremendous experience for little John. He rode on one of his father's two horses or walked beside the front pair of oxen; sometimes he herded the cattle together, and when he was tired he rested under the white tilt of the wagon, along with his mother and the smaller children. Towards sunset his eyes would wander longingly over the landscape, in the hope of discovering a good camping-place before his father did. And when the rattling wagon finally stopped, he was the first to look for water and for sticks for the fire. While his mother cooked the dinner, he helped his father; the animals had to be given water and tied up for the night. At night he preferred to sleep outside the wagon, on the ground, rolled up in his blanket, while the eyes of wild beasts glowed in the darkness about the burning camp fire.

After a whole summer of travelling, they reached the Mississippi. There they settled down. Not far from the frontier town of St Louis, Father Sager staked out some land, cleared it, ploughed it, built a log house on it. And so they had a farm again. John hunted and fished, wandered round with an old rifle in his hand. He caught a raccoon and tamed it, learnt the habits of animals and how to mimic the sounds they made. He could coo like a wood pigeon, screech like an owl, and squawk like a wild turkey; he could howl like a coyote and he could imitate the hoarse bellowing of a deer in spring. He got to know the Indians, whom he saw come on their ponies, wrapped in blankets, to trade with the white settlers. He also took part in skirmishes and learnt to fight; he was not often frightened.

But he was not destined to grow up in that region. When he was a bit over thirteen years old, his father was seized with the desire to go on. Henry Sager had the nature of a true pioneer; he wanted to explore, he wanted to see and reclaim new land, he wanted to join with other pioneers in making America great. But the work of such men as he was risky. The Indians did not look meekly on while their ancestral hunting-grounds were destroyed by the white people; and Nature in that wilderness of the Far West was cruel, treacherous, dangerous – though fabulously beautiful. Henry Sager was drawn by that wondrous land as by a magnet. Hitherto he had not dared to give way to temptation; his family was a large one, and the journey was perilous. But the previous summer – that was to say, in 1843 – a great caravan of emigrants had gone for the first time to Oregon, in the north-west. That summer another caravan was to go; and he had the opportunity of selling his land and his farmhouse to newcomers from the east for a good price. This time he felt he could take the risk. The future of his children would lie in that splendid country yonder; through them, America would become great, his dream would become reality.

When they went, John was thirteen years and eight months old.

A. RUTGERS VAN DER LOEFF

The Chief Characters in This Story

FATHER, HENRY SAGER: a man with little wiry curls above a hard neck, and shrewd eyes wrinkled-up in a keen, red-brown face. Strong as a bear, and brave. He has an unshakable belief in Providence. The children have an unshakable belief in him – 'Father can do everything'; perhaps he can also conquer Oregon and make it great.

MOTHER, NAOMI SAGER: sweet-natured and compliant. On Sundays she wears a shawl of purple silk with a long fringe. She has big eyes as black as velvet. She sits under the cover of the ox wagon wearing a straw sunbonnet, a green-striped cotton jacket, and a black woollen skirt.

JOHN: thirteen years old, nearly fourteen, looks like Father, but is fairer. Because Father believes in Providence, John believes in it a little bit as well, but at present Father is the sole object of his blind worship. He loves the beauty and gentleness of his mother; is an out-and-out man.

FRANCIS: just turned eleven, looks like Mother, has a fund of dogged, very great courage deep in his heart. He is not so strong as John, and is slightly built and dark. He admires his brother, but he does his level best not to show it.

LOUISE: twelve years old, a careful, self-sacrificing soul. Good, perhaps a little too good, always tidying up and horribly neat.

CATHERINE: nine years old, the 'tummy-ache child', full of plans, ideas, excuses, and silly fibs. She has dark-red, untidy hair, is a little bit vain and inclined to be lazy.

MATILDA: five years old, nearly six. A quiet child who is very fond of animals and gets on remarkably well with them.

ELIZABETH or LIZZY: a plucky little toddler of three. Sometimes seen with big tears rolling down her cheeks. Is spoilt by everyone, especially by Louise.

BABY INDEPENTIA: not yet baptised.

ANNA: a Durham (shorthorn) cow. An excellent, strong beast, with big, brown, gentle eyes. Two years old.

WALTER: an ox, also of the genuine Durham breed. A heavy, strong animal, but older than Anna, and owing to his weight his hooves are more liable to split on the long journey.

OSCAR: a wolf dog.

1

The River Laramie flowed wild and roaring, broad and foaming, through the green, hilly landscape; but, in that dry season, it was nowhere more than about three feet deep. Here and there spikes of rock stuck up in it, over which the water splashed and spattered, and the low banks were also stony and rough. Willows grew along it, and here and there thickets of cottonwood trees.

Somewhat higher up the valley, towards the foot of the first hills, lay Fort Laramie.

It was an oblong, low building, with a palisade of wooden posts on top of the stone walls. Those outer walls formed the rear side of all the rooms in the fort, which opened on to the inner courtyard. The courtyard was square; its floor was of stamped earth, and almost white in the scorching noonday sun. To reach it you had to go through a gate in a massive, square tower pierced with openings for guns.

It was a good, strong fort, in which the factor and his sixteen men could feel safe. Besides, they often gave hospitality to soldiers of Government expeditions in transit. And that was the case now. Fort Laramie, alone in the wilderness, six hundred and sixty-seven miles from the last outpost of the inhabited world, was the principal trading-point on the route to Oregon and California.

On this blazing afternoon in June 1844 not a man

was to be seen in the courtyard.

The only person about was an Indian woman, who was sitting in a corner under an awning, sewing a pair of moccasins, while a little half-breed child beside her played with a handful of beads. Almost everyone had retired indoors, to try to take an afternoon nap in the comparative coolness between the adobe walls.

Alone in the office, two clerks of the American Fur Company were hunched yawning at their high desks, sending their goose quills scratching over the paper on which they were drawing up, in fair round figures and letters, an inventory of the fort's stock of food. A big caravan of emigrants was expected to arrive shortly, and then it would be important to know what you had in the house.

Through the open door the sound of men's voices filtered into the room, and the younger of the two clerks, who was more at home in the saddle than at the ledger, now and then cast a longing look outside, where three men sat talking together – not in the hot courtyard, but under the cool arch of the gate in the tower. One of them was Thomas Fitzpatrick, the famous guide and trapper, who knew as few others did the enormous expanse of the Rocky Mountains and the wilderness to the east and west of them.

Fitzpatrick was busy telling the factor, Boudeau, and the officer commanding the small detachment of Government troops how he had managed to dodge groups of Sioux Indians on the warpath on his way from the Rockies to the fort, when a little Indian on a prairie pony came storming in through the gate and shouted something unintelligible.

At once, the American soldiers in their blue and red uniforms, the trappers in their leather breeches and jerkins, and some Indian women and children, came flocking into the square through the open doors, from all sides.

It appeared that the strange rider was a Dakota Indian, who had come to say that his whole village was on its way there because the train of emigrants would arrive very soon. Scouts had given them the information. The Dakotas' chief 'Five Crows' intended to ask the emigrants to invite his people to a feast.

'Hm,' muttered Fitzpatrick, who had remained calmly sitting on his rough wooden crate in the shade of the gateway. 'I've seen them feasts before. They're nothing but barefaced robbery. All them darned Indians are out for is to get the last few pounds of coffee and flour out of the poor, exhausted slobs. Cruelty to animals, that's what it is! And if the perishers don't get their way, worse things happen. A farmer who hits the trail for the wilderness is the craziest creature on two legs.'

He knocked his pipe out, took his tobacco pouch, and began to fill a new pipe for himself, now and again casting a jaundiced eye at the excited throng in the courtyard.

The landscape round the fort was still quiet and deserted.

He went on grumbling:

'. . . a farmer who hits the trail for the wilderness with cattle and plough and a wagon full of squalling kids is the craziest creature on earth. Those suckers do just about every silly thing they can do. At night they leave their saddles and harness hanging up outside, and next morning all they find is rags of leather, gnawed to bits by the coyotes. They don't know how to keep their cattle together, and at night their guards nod off to sleep, and leave the road wide open for Indian horse thieves. Greenhorns, that's what they are, who don't know the first thing about anything! They overload their wagons, and on the rocky ground the axles break like matchsticks; they get drowned in cloudbursts, they get lost in sandstorms, and if there should be a tiny patch of quicksand anywhere, you can bet your boots *they'll* get stuck in it. They catch fever when they drink water from buffalo pools, and they get the pip if they have to live on anything else but coffee and cake and fat bacon. It's a sheer miracle any of 'em reach the other side of the mountains alive . . .'

'Man!' shouted Boudeau, suddenly appearing beside him with upraised arms. 'There they are!'

It was not the emigrants; it was the Indians.

Within a few minutes the hills on the other side of the river were covered with a disorderly horde of savages, on horseback, and on foot. The foremost of them had already reached the bank, and plunged into the foaming water. In the twinkling of an eye, the river was alive with dogs, horses, and human beings.

On either side of the rough packsaddles on the horses, which were heaped high with household goods, long poles were fastened. The ends of the poles dragged along the ground, and a little way behind the tail of the horse, baskets had been suspended between the poles, in which baggage had been piled – or, as often as not, a litter of squealing puppies or a clutch of screaming brown babies or, now and again, a very old man. Many of those baskets were now splashing across the river, and between the horses dogs were swimming. The grown men on horseback, the 'warriors', shot like lightning through the mob, some with a slender Indian boy sitting beside them. The women sat on top of the packsaddles, or waded along on foot. The chaos was indescribable.

The entire cavalcade came swarming up the bank on the other side; stray horses and young foals ran loose through the turmoil, screamed after by the women who were supposed to take care of them.

The uproar did not last long; silence fell fairly suddenly when every family – complete with horses, dogs, children, pots, and pans – had reached the flat, open space behind the fort and begun to pitch its tents.

In less than an hour, sixty tepees were standing there. Several hundred horses were grazing on the surrounding prairie, and dogs were running all over the place. The men approached the fort; small children shouted and screamed right under its walls.

The inhabitants of the fort had not yet recovered

from the tumult, when Boudeau suddenly bawled to his Indian wife to bring him his spyglass. He stood on the wall looking through it for a couple of minutes.

Pointing to the east, he shouted:

'By thunder, there come the emigrants!'

It was some time before they could be seen with the naked eye; four long columns of ox wagons with white covers, jostled by a sea of thousands of head of cattle, and men on horseback – a laboriously moving caravan stubbornly forging ahead against the misty blue background of rolling hills in the east.

'There they are, them there backwoods farmers on the prairie, them lapdogs in the lion's den, them poor tender-feet in the wilderness of the West!' Fitzpatrick grumbled beside Boudeau.

An hour later, the first wagons had reached the river; without halting or hesitating for a moment, they plunged in, heavily, awkwardly. Slowly and sluggishly the draught oxen waded through the strongly flowing water until it came right up to their dewlaps, after which they laboriously climbed up the opposite bank. The drivers shouted and cracked their whips; the wagons rumbled lurching and swaying over the river's stony strand.

The caravan made straight for the fort, until it almost reached the gate, when the wagons wheeled round in a circle and stopped.

For some time, all was quiet. The emigrants were preparing their camp. But no sooner had they finished doing that than the fort was, as it were, taken by storm.

A crowd of lean, suntanned faces under broad-brimmed hats suddenly appeared before the gate. Staring eyes – exclamations of amazement – tears, in the case of some of the women. They had covered nearly seven hundred miles, and in all that time they had not seen a table or chair. After the long, exhausting journey through the totally unknown prairie wilderness – after all the privations and brushes with Indian cattle thieves, this was the first patch of white civilisation they had come across. And it would be about the last . . .

Broad-shouldered men, in coarse, homespun clothing; thin women's faces under sunbonnets, with black rings round their eyes – figures with weary, drooping shoulders in woollen jackets and wide, dark shirts; children whose eyes nearly bolted from their heads with curiosity and longing . . . the whole crowd pressed inside, excitedly talking, to explore every nook and corner of the fort. With open mouths they looked at the fat Indian squaws with their greasy, blue-black hair, who had retreated soundlessly and swiftly and were now staring back inquisitively, from the corners of the rooms in which they evidently lived, at the gaping intruders in the doorways.

In a stentorian voice, Boudeau shouted a command from the inner courtyard. The men shrugged their shoulders irritatedly; but well . . . if it had to be, they would do as he wanted them to do, and send their women and children back to camp. If it came to that, it really would be better if they, the menfolk, did business, obtained advice, and discussed problems alone.

That night a group of men sat talking in the courtyard of Fort Laramie, in the delicious cool of evening and with a view through the open gate of a scarlet sunset above the hills.

Without exception, their faces were serious, almost sombre. The guide, the factor, and two trappers were telling the pioneers what the remainder of their journey would be like.

'From now on, you'll find next to no grass for your cattle, and you'll meet precious few buffalo. What are you going to live on, and how do you propose to get those heavy wagons over the mountains with your oxen weakened as they are?'

'What Dr Whitman did last year with *his* caravan, we can do too. In fact, we can do it more easily, because he's blazed the trail for us. Our wagons will follow the tracks of his; that's how we'll get there, and that's how many will get there after us. The valleys of Oregon will be occupied by our people, and our children will be happy there.'

It was Henry Sager who said that and he spoke with such strength of conviction that the sneer even died from the lips of that hard-bitten prairieman and mountain-hunter Fitzpatrick.

But the men in whose name Sager spoke continued to look gloomy.

They had been travelling for forty days now from their starting-point, Independence, Missouri. The ecstasy of 'prairie fever', which seized almost everyone who rode for the first time through those endlessly rolling, blossoming, and fragrant green prospects, had given way to a certain melancholy; the vast buffalo plains had followed, covered with dry manure, and manure, and still more manure, with here and there bleached bones and pools of mud dried up to crusts. The short, crisp, curling grass had formed good food for the cattle; but the pioneers had also travelled through regions of shifting sand dunes and waterless deserts, where at night the fires of buffalo manure had cast a spectral glow on disconsolate faces, while the cattle lowed wretchedly round the camp. Indians had filched their cattle and horses from them, and men had been killed in the rearguard.

The emigrants were disheartened by the rigours and disappointments of their arduous journey; the hooves of many of the animals were so worn that they could hardly get along on them. At that rate, what was the future going to be like? For they had not yet covered half the route, and the worst part was still to come.

'Leave some of your cattle behind here. In their place, you can have packhorses and mules from us, and we'll let you have some coffee and sugar as well,' Boudeau suggested.

Coffee and sugar . . . coffee and sugar . . . if anyone had told them three months before that they would one day barter their precious cattle for coffee and sugar they would have given him a rough answer. But now . . . coffee and sugar had a wondrous attraction.

And the feast the Dakotas were extorting from them also stuck in their gullets – they would need extra supplies for that, anyway. But they dared not refuse to offer it.

'With your train of heavy wagons, you're too vulnerable to attacks by Indians, too,' said one of the trappers. 'They're growing more and more hostile. They're beginning to feel that the white invasion's getting beyond a joke. If the Government doesn't take a stronger line soon, we'll have no end of trouble here.'

Fitzpatrick shook his grey head and laid a mahogany-coloured, weatherbeaten hand on Henry Sager's arm. He bent forward, so that the long fringe of his buckskin trapper's jerkin dangled over the table.

'You people don't tackle the Indians sensibly,' he said quietly. 'You only encourage them by being so nervous. That way, you expose yourselves to real danger. But show 'em your teeth; be vigilant, bold – look as though you believed in yourselves when they're by, and you'll see that they'll make quite decent neighbours. But your safety depends on the respect you manage to inspire. And that's a fact.'

The others said nothing. It was wise advice, but not easy to follow.

Those farmers on the trail were anything but themselves. Most of them burned with a bold and enterprising spirit, but they belonged in the forests, on a farm; they felt lost on the limitless prairie, on the desolate, high buffalo plains, and among the mountains. They were as different from genuine trappers as a seaman differs from a French-Canadian *voyageur*, bobbing and dancing in his canoe in the rapids of the mountain rivers. They were brave, but they were ignorant and inexperienced; they knew nothing of the country and its wild inhabitants. They had already had many misfortunes and they would have still more.

'Some of us have drunk bad water,' said one of the emigrants, a young man with a full red beard. His eyes were the most wretched of them all. 'My wife's died of it.'

'Dysentery?' asked Fitzpatrick brusquely.

The young man nodded. He swallowed, and suddenly walked off, out through the gate, to the camp of covered wagons.

'He's got a child – a little girl of three years old,' said one of the others. The men belonging to the fort had glanced at each other. Dysentery . . . perhaps cholera. Risk of infection. The sooner those emigrants went on their way, the better.

'If I was you,' said the factor, 'I'd push on ahead like nobody's business. You've still got a long way to go, and you want to reach your destination before winter sets in. As far as Fort Hall, the journey'll be comfortable enough. But take my advice – leave some of your cattle behind, buy some horses instead, and, if possible, convert some of your heavy wagons into two-wheeled carts, so that you'll be able to get along more quickly and more lightly.'

'We'll think about it,' said Henry Sager pensively.

★   ★   ★

The following night, the feast for the Indians took place.

The women, although they were tired out, had had to bake cakes and bread, and their eyes smarted from the smoke of the fires. The men sat calculating how much tobacco they would have to give up. But the children nearly went off their heads with joy. It had been so long since they had had any celebrations, and there had been such delicious smells in the air all day.

Round the Sager family's wagon was a tremendous stir and bustle. All the children had had to put red flannel shirts on. Mother and Louise had already washed the dirty ones; they hung flapping from clothes lines between the cottonwood trees.

John buckled his belt of snakeskin tight, and felt for the hunting knife at his hip. Yes . . . there it was; you never knew what might happen. Francis, who was eleven years old, dark and slightly built, followed John everywhere; John, with his fair, sturdy head and shoulders looked more like fifteen than thirteen. Louise had washed and combed her long, light-brown hair, and was now running around with a couple of soaking wet plaits, looking for Lizzy. Lizzy had to be washed and combed too, but she had smelt the water and, as usual, had fled as far as her fat, unsteady little legs would carry her. Catherine was supposed to be helping to look for her, but she didn't want to. Red with the exertion, she sat pulling at her short, dark-red curls, through which it was impossible to get a comb.

Louise was in charge of things at the wagon, for Mother was on duty at one of the three big fires on which the coffee was being made.

John had offered to go and work at the fire in his mother's place. He did not care for that women's nonsense round the coffee kettles, but he had seen how unwell his mother felt; she had been deathly pale these last few days, her eyes looked even larger and blacker than usual, and this morning she had been so dizzy when she lifted the bacon tub in the wagon that she had almost fallen down. Nevertheless, she had refused to accept John's offer.

'I'd sooner you helped Louise with the babies,' she had said.

Well . . . to trail around behind those children – that was a thing that went *right* against the grain. Good Lord – look at Cathie tugging at her hair! He went up and gave her a dig in the ribs.

'Come off it – you're quite beautiful enough!'

'Ow, you nasty boy,' she cried and lashed out at him with a lean brown leg from under her red shirt.

He stood there laughing; and the expression in his eyes was so much that of a friendly man's that Cathie shook her curls down over her face and went on with her attempts to bring some order into them.

John strolled round the wagon and his family like a sheepdog round his sheep. Francis, feeling that he had had enough, sat down in the grass, chewed a bit of stick, and contented himself with following John with his eyes.

Suddenly they heard a noise. It was time, too. The

Indians were coming, and abruptly Lizzy appeared, running and howling; with a fiery red little face which was so screwed up with crying that it looked all mouth and creases, and with bent arms outstretched, she ran straight into John's safe, red-flannel arms. He snatched her up, and in a flash the spectacle ceased to be terrifying to her.

With faces full of expectation, the Indians came into the camp: old men with grey hair done up in a bun, 'warriors' in peace costume, youths, women, and children, colourfully dressed. They all sat down, wrapped in their blankets, in a semicircle, with the chief in the middle and his warriors on either side of him; then came the 'braves' and the youths, and finally the squaws with the children. Coffee and cake was put in front of them. Before the emigrants knew where it had gone, everything had disappeared, to the accompaniment of loud shouts and vehement gestures of satisfaction.

More cake! With open mouths, the white people stood gaping at their wild guests. Out of sheer wanton frolicsomeness the latter threw down the coffee cups – perhaps the last there were – and smashed them to pieces. One emigrant reached for his rifle; a woman laid her hand on his wrist.

'Hotheads are no use to us here – we don't want to land from the frying pan into the fire,' the voice of one of the oldest pioneers called imperiously.

The Indians feasted, danced, shouted, and sang. The whites looked on. The sun went down. Dark clouds hung above the hills.

There, where the sun had sunk behind that black bank of clouds – there was the West, there lay their future, there they would go, despite all difficulties. This meeting with the Dakotas, who had journeyed for a week to collect a cup of coffee and a slice of cake, had gone off peacefully at any rate.

Three days later, the emigrants went on their way.

They had had a bit of a rest. Seven of the sixty-nine wagons had been converted into two-wheeled carts. Some of the cattle remained behind; and in their place Boudeau had supplied thirty-five packhorses and sixteen mules with packsaddles – they did not look as if they were of the best – and some coffee and sugar. He rubbed his hands with glee. Such magnificent cattle – some of them were real Durhams – normally cost the earth there.

Fitzpatrick stood watching the caravan go; his lip curled contemptuously: 'You're too sharp for my liking, pal. Those horses won't stand the pace in the mountains. Haven't the poor wretches got a hard enough time ahead of them, without you making it harder? Sakes alive, the trouble's started already!'

Just before the last column of the long train of jolting, swaying ox wagons disappeared from sight, the axle of one of the vehicles evidently broke. The wagon lurched, and slewed half round.

'You see! Their equipment's no good. In terrain like this, the strongest still isn't strong enough.'

Furious, he walked back in through the gate; then turned and looked once more at the people out there, milling like ants round that broken-down wagon. Again he saw red. He had wanted to help them; but how?

2

From Fort Laramie, which lay in the fork between the Laramie and North Platte rivers, the caravan followed the bow-shaped course of the North Platte.

Often, however, they were several miles away from it. It was difficult to find the best terrain for the wagons; the hills were steep, and the ground was littered with enormous boulders and pebbles. The guide, who rode in front, kept his men busy galloping to and fro to search out the most suitable route. Nevertheless, they made good time; the scenery was beautiful, the sky unusually clear, and the air at that high altitude was bracingly fresh, in spite of the hot sun. They went higher and higher. Before them lay the tremendous peaks and ridges of the Rocky Mountains.

Towards nightfall they generally managed to find a perfectly satisfactory camping-place, with good grass for the animals, running water, and wood for the fires. Day's journeys of seventeen and eighteen miles were nothing out of the ordinary. That was fine.

No further mishaps had occurred since the one accident, immediately after they had left Fort Laramie, in which the Ford family's wagon had been so badly damaged that it was only fit for the scrapheap. The Fords and their belongings had been distributed among other wagons, and Mrs Ford had joined the Sagers in their wagon, because Mrs Sager was expecting a baby any day.

The farther and higher they went, the less grass grew; the landscape looked nothing like that splendid, blossoming, rolling prairie of the first weeks of their journey. Nor did it resemble the hard, dry buffalo plains which they had subsequently taken weeks to cross. There was more timber now, though, and hence they no longer had to depend chiefly on dried buffalo droppings for fuel for their fires.

Over and over again, it was necessary to cross some wide, muddy creek of the River Platte. But there were always places which could be easily forded. However, it was a more difficult matter to cross the broad, swiftly flowing river itself, as they had to do early one morning.

The water there was higher than it had been in the Laramie; the guide and his men repeatedly galloped their horses into the stream while the front of the caravan stood waiting on the bank; but there was no ford to be found. They would have to swim for it. Someone would have to take over to the other side the line along which the wagons would be able to cross the river like ferryboats. It was a dangerous job, because treacherously sucking whirlpools eddied and boiled in the middle of the broad stream. There came a blast on the bugle: volunteers forward!

John Sager was sitting on the bank. He had tied his horse beside him to a willow shrub, and he was biting with clenched teeth the stem of an empty pipe of his father's which he had upside down in his mouth. If only he was older! He knew for certain that they would not give *him* a chance.

Volunteers forward!

Nobody came forward. But John's face cleared when he suddenly saw his father advancing to the front; his father was riding a good horse which was very capable of holding its own against the current.

But voices of protest went up.

A couple of older men walked towards Henry Sager. As father of a large family, they did not want him to run such a risk.

Then a little black mustang came galloping up from the rear of the caravan. Its rider was Walton, the young man with the big red beard who had lost his wife. As he dashed past he seized the rope from the hands of Sager, who was all ready to set out, and drove his horse into the river.

The point on the other bank directly opposite the wagon train did not seem to be a bad landing-place. But Walton went into the water at an angle against the current, for in the middle the river would no doubt drive him and his horse downstream.

The horse was swimming now, its head was bobbing regularly up and down. The man was swimming beside it; his red hair looked like a wig floating on the water. In his headlong haste he had forgotten to throw his hat off; it was floating swiftly downstream — was, in fact, already almost out of sight.

What a long time it took! And then, to think – on top of that, all the people, animals, wagons, and carts would have to cross too, presently. John sat looking on in acute suspense. But his father called to him. He had to come and help. The men had begun to prepare the vehicles for crossing. The oxen were being unyoked.

Suddenly a shout of joy went up from a little group of women and children who were standing on the bank. Man and horse had reached the other side. Walton was now busy making the line fast. He signalled that the crossing could begin.

The wagons were coupled to each other, and one by one they rumbled along the rope into the water, after which, like so many floating arks, with women, children, and household bits and pieces, they began to slide across to the other side.

Now it was the turn of the cattle. The first oxen went into the water upstream from the wagons. At the head went five men, each on the downstream side of one ox. They held one hand against its withers and swam with the other, prodding and urging the ungainly animal to keep to a straight line, in spite of the powerful current. Men on horseback were driving the other cattle into the water; more than two thousand cows, oxen, mules, and horses with riders were swimming across the broad river in six or seven rows beside each other. When the foremost were more than halfway, hundreds were still standing waiting on the bank.

John was one of those foremost. He had asked his father whether he might be allowed to go with their oxen.

'Father – I can do it! Really I can! And Mary's a splendid swimmer.'

He patted Mary's shining neck.

His father had glanced at him thoughtfully. Then he had said: 'Right, lad.'

John had seen his mother's pallid face in the shade of the grey-white cover of their wagon. Her dark eyes were full of worry, but she said nothing. Francis, sitting beside her, looked at him admiringly. But Louise, behind them, had called out in her old wife's fashion:

'You'll be careful, John, won't you?'

As he trotted off, he had turned in the saddle and put his tongue out at her. Then he had blushed for shame at such childish behavior. A man driving cattle across a river doesn't put his tongue out.

Mary swam splendidly. John felt almost uncomfortably safe on her back. It was like crossing the river on a sofa. The oxen swam well too. Only Charley seemed uneasy. John had had trouble in even getting him into the water.

When they were nearly halfway across, the animal began to drift downstream, in the direction of the wagons. John spurred his horse, and Mary was soon swimming beside the ox.

Charley became even more restive.

John took a quick decision; he slid from the saddle, and the horse went on, swimming more swiftly without him. He reached out for the ox's head, but before he realized what was happening, a whirlpool sucked both of them down.

After a terrible moment of black suffocation, he rose to the surface again; he gasped for breath, he gulped for air, but all he got was a mouthful of water. He was choking, his lungs seemed on the point of cracking, there was a bursting pain in his chest, his heart thumped. He swam with wild strokes, blindly, until he felt himself seized by another whirlpool, which again sucked him deep down below the surface.

Without knowing why, he suddenly thought of Louise, at whom he had put out his tongue, and of his mother's white face, and his father's piercing brown eyes as they had looked at him just now, searchingly and yet full of confidence.

Now he was going to drown, and he would never see them again, not Francis, or Cathie, or Lizzy, or anyone else . . . anyone . . . suddenly he felt something heavy bump against him down in the water. His hand groped for support there – it was the hairy shank of his ox; he rose to the surface along the animal's side, discovering that it was now swimming at an angle against the current, evidently trying to rejoin the herd.

John remained swimming beside its head, occasionally glancing gratefully at the mild, frightened eyes of the beast. He had wanted to rescue Charley, and it was Charley who had rescued him.

On the other bank, Mary was waiting patiently for him. She had got almost dry already, in the sun. She was nibbling at a big tuft of grass in the shade of a red willow. John did not get on to her back. He hardly glanced up or around, and threw himself down in the grass beside his horse, who bowed her head over him for a moment; then he shut his eyes. An hour later his father found him there, fast asleep.

The great trek went on.

They passed the picturesque 'Red Buttes' – two high, round rocks, on their left side. There the river flowed through a deep canyon, the 'Fiery Narrows', where some years before a Government expedition had been cut to pieces in a bitter fight with the Indians.

Their route took them higher, through a wild, barren region. Not everyone among them could stand the mountain air so well. Only now and again did they find a spring; and, even then, the water was usually strongly alkaline, and had an unpleasant taste.

The guide kept their courage up by painting exquisite pictures of a camping-place which was only a couple of days' journey away: at Willow Creek Spring – there they would be able to rest for a few days; there was good grass there for the cattle, there was fresh water, and the women would be able to do some washing. At night, in the darkness of wagon or tent, when the children were asleep, the men put heart into the women in their turn.

Only two more days, only one more day . . .

That day began like any other.

At four o'clock in the morning, when the rising sun stood like a red-glowing ball above the grey landscape, the guards fired off their rifles, as a sign that the hours of sleep were past. Women, men, and children streamed out of every tent and wagon; the gently smouldering fires from the previous night were replenished with wood, and bluish-grey clouds from dozens of plumes of smoke began to float through the morning air.

Bacon was fried, coffee was made, by those who still had some. The families which could still cook maize mush for the children thought themselves lucky.

All this took place within the 'corral', that was to say inside the ring which had been made by driving the wagons into a circle and fastening them firmly to each other by means of the shafts and chains. This formed a strong barricade through which even the most vicious ox could not break, and in the event of an attack by the Sioux Indians it would be a bulwark that was not to be despised.

Outside the corral the cattle and horses cropped the sparse grass in a wide circle.

At five o'clock sixty men mounted their horses and rode out of the camp. They fanned out through the crowds of cattle until they reached the outskirts of the herd; once there, they encircled the herd and began to drive all the cattle before them. The trained animals knew what those cracking whips meant, and what was required of them, and moved slowly in the direction of the camp. There the drivers picked their teams of oxen out from the dense mass and led them into the corral, where the yoke was put upon them.

From six o'clock until seven, the camp was extra busy; breakfast was eaten, tents were struck, wagons were loaded, and the teams of draught oxen and mules were made ready to be harnessed to their respective wagons and carts, Everyone knew that whoever was not ready when the signal to start was blown at seven o'clock would be doomed for that day to travel in the dusty rear of the caravan.

There were sixty-eight vehicles. They were divided into seventeen columns, each consisting of four wagons and carts. Each column, took it in turn to lead the way. The section that was at the head today would bring up the rear tomorrow, unless a driver had missed his place in the row through laziness or negligence, and had to travel behind by way of punishment.

It was ten minutes to seven.

There were gaps everywhere in the corral; the teams of oxen were being harnessed in front of the wagons, the chains clanked. The women and children had taken their places under the canvas covers. The guide was standing among his assistants at the head of the line, ready to mount his horse and show the way. A dozen young men who were not on duty that day formed another group. They were going out buffalo-hunting; they had good horses and were well armed, which was certainly necessary, for the hostile Sioux had driven the herds of buffalo away from the River Platte, so that the hunters would be forced to ride fifteen or twenty miles to reach them.

As soon as the herdsmen were ready, they hurried to the rear of their herd, in order to drive them together and get them ready for today's march.

Seven o'clock.

An end had come to the busy running and walking to and fro, the cracking of whips, the shouts of command to the oxen, and the bawling from wagon to wagon – in short, to everything which, only just now, had appeared to be complete and utter chaos. Every driver was at his post. A bugle rang out! The guide and his escort mounted their horses; the four wagons of the leading section rumbled out of the camp and formed the first column, the rest took their places with the regularity of clockwork, and the caravan moved slowly forward over the broad plateau, far above the foaming river.

A new, hard day had begun. Particularly hard for the Sagers, who were having to do without the help of Mrs Ford, since she had gone to look after Walton's sick child.

The sun rose high in the sky. It was hot and stuffy under the canvas tilts, which were thick with dust. Towards noon the children everywhere began to bicker and whimper. But in the Sager family's wagon, they had other things to worry about.

John, who had been riding for hours in the blazing sun, beside the heads of the foremost yoke of oxen, was given an order by his father, who was sitting on the driver's bench in the front of the wagon.

Immediately he galloped forward.

He had to fetch the doctor.

The doctor was a veterinary surgeon; the emigrants did not have a real doctor with them. But the vet had already done people a great deal of good, and helped them considerably, as well as animals.

John rode with all his might. Why on earth didn't the doctor travel in the middle of the caravan? From his father's face the boy had seen that the matter was urgent.

Meanwhile, Henry Sager had driven his wagon out of the line. He stopped.

'All the children must get out,' he ordered. 'Go and collect buffalo droppings and make a fire. Louise has to boil as much water as she can.'

Before Louise left the wagon, she filled the big kettle with water, scooping it up in a little tin bowl from the barrel in the back of the wagon. She cast a timid glance at her mother, who lay still and white on the tarpaulin. Mother caught Louise's eye and gave her a gentle, encouraging nod. If only that doctor would come quickly!

The doctor came.

With his long legs, he stepped from the saddle into the wagon in one stride. John tied up his horse. Then he wiped the sweat and dust out of his eyes with the back of his hand.

To the children, it seemed to take a long time. The water had already been boiling for quite a while. No one had asked for it yet, and they did not dare to look into the wagon.

In the distance ahead of them hung a thick cloud of dust, behind which the caravan was hidden. They would fall very far to the rear. John look worried. He knew that that was dangerous – stragglers ran the risk of being attacked; but he said nothing. Now and again his father came out and glanced around, scanned the trail behind them – eight sets of wagon wheels beside each other and thousands upon thousands of hoof marks. But behind, the horizon was clear and empty.

Until John suddenly perceived a tiny cloud of dust.

He started. He knew that that could only mean that Indians were approaching.

'Father!' he shouted.

Henry Sager stuck his head out of the wagon.

John pointed to the east, where the cloud of dust above their own tracks had now grown rather larger.

Father Sager said nothing.

He went back into the wagon with the kettle of boiling water, but came out again a moment later with five rifles and two pistols. John had already pulled his own pistol from its holster. His father gave him a rifle.

'All the children except John and Louise, get under the wagon,' he commanded quietly. But it was easy to see that that calmness of his required all the self-control he had. His strong, wrinkled neck was fiery red, and the veins on his forehead were thick and purple.

'Take these,' he said to his eldest daughter, and Louise stood with three rifles in her arms, staring at the approaching cloud of dust as if turned to stone.

Father put the powder horn, lead, and ramrods down beside her.

John had laid his rifle across the saddlebow in front of him, as he had always seen the trappers do.

But his father said:

'Are you mad, boy? Get down and tie Mary up in front, along with the oxen. Do you want to serve as a target, and be shot out of the saddle?'

Francis pushed the smaller children under the wagon. Catherine began to resist, crying and kicking. 'Stop howling, you little idiot,' Francis snapped nervously, trying to make his voice sound as manly as possible. Matilda and Lizzy thought it rather a nice game; as a rule, they were never allowed to go under the wagon.

Father Sager climbed back in again.

He brought out two empty water casks, and the only bag of flour they had left. He stood the two casks upright beside the wagon, near one of the rear wheels, and laid the sack of flour across them.

'Come to the back here,' he ordered John and Louise. 'And remember – don't stir from cover. We fire along to one side of this, and between the casks. . . . Louise, you load the rifles when we've fired them,' he said to her. To John he said nothing; he only looked at him.

A sound came from the wagon. It was like the crying of a tiny baby.

Father Sager gritted his teeth, and behaved as if he had not heard anything. The sound came again, more distinctly this time. Then he looked at his two eldest children; he almost had tears in his eyes.

'May God help us to protect that young life,' he said between clenched teeth. Rather more calmly, he went on: 'If it comes to that, it's not certain that the Indians mean mischief. And our rifles are good, sound ones. John, don't fire too soon, let 'em get close.'

He put his head back into the wagon.

'Don't worry, Doctor – we'll call if we can't manage without you.'

They waited in suspense. It was now easy to see that the cause of the cloud was horsemen – not many, perhaps half a dozen, Indians on prairie ponies. They were superior in numbers, but they could not take cover anywhere.

There was no brushwood in which they could ensconce themselves.

'May God help us to protect that young life,' Father had said.

Those words made an indelible impression on John.

There, inside the wagon, a new brother or sister was lying – they did not even know yet which it was; but it was a new life, and it was theirs. It had been given to them to take care of. Mother had had so much trouble to bring it into the world, and now Father and he had to see to it that . . . just imagine, suppose something should happen to it!

John got even hotter than he was already. He pushed his hat to the back of his head, and wiped his dusty, sweaty face with his sleeve for the umpteenth time. He spat on the ground.

During the ride up to the front of the caravan to fetch the doctor, he had felt as if he was biting the dust that had been stirred up. If only it would rain! Queer, that . . . that he should think of rain at this moment.

The Indians were so close now that he could see that one of them was carrying a rifle; the others had bows and arrows.

There . . . the first arrow came whizzing through the air. Its iron tip bored through the canvas cover of the wagon; the feathered tail stood buzzing and quivering.

A shot rang out, but Father motioned to John to hold his hand.

Then . . . they both fired at the same time.

The foremost Indian, the one with the rifle, fell

sideways from his horse, wounded. The animal dragged him a short distance along the ground. The other members of the troop swerved away immediately, rode round in a great circle at tremendous speed, and charged again.

Once more Henry and John Sager fired their two rifles, while the arrows whistled above their heads.

Number two was shot out of the saddle. One of his comrades seized him just in time, and pulled him on to his horse, in front of him.

John's hat was whipped from his head; a dry tap sounded; he glanced round. An arrow had drilled its way deep into the woodwork of the wagon, carrying hat and all. Then he heard a splash – he just glimpsed the arms of the doctor, who had emptied a bowl of water out through the tilt.

Louise pushed another freshly loaded rifle into his hands. But it was no longer necessary. The Indians had now picked up the first of their two wounded, and were galloping off in a wide arc. The two riderless ponies were running far away in the distance. Soon there was nothing to be seen but slowly settling dust.

'Indian cattle thieves,' said father Sager brusquely. 'They'll have been disappointed.'

He took the sack of flour and climbed into the wagon with it. An arrow had pierced it; a white trail of its precious contents was trickling down through a little hole.

A moment later he stuck his head outside again:

'You can all come in,' he said solemnly.

One by one they climbed into the wagon, John

leading the way. He tried to behave very sedately, but inwardly he was trembling. Louise had John's hat in her hands, and was trying to smooth out the dents in it. Cathie gave Francis a push, so that he nearly fell on his face as he climbed in; that was her way of revenging herself for just now. Stretching out his long arms in their striped flannel shirt sleeves, Henry Sager lifted Matilda and Lizzy from the ground.

The red of all those children's shirts, so bright in the sun outside, became dark in the darkness of the wagon. And there lay Mother, like a beautiful picture in black and white, her pale face with those much too big eyes laughing sweetly up at them, and her long dark hair spread out on both sides of her head against the white canvas. The doctor threw away a last bowl of water, dried his hands, and gave Father Sager a hearty slap on the back. Only then did the children see that Father was holding something in his arms. It was a baby washed and combed, with a big forelock of black hair but for the rest looking ridiculously tiny in Mother's purple silk shawl.

'She'll weigh a about nine pounds, I guess – an enormous child!' said the doctor.

An enormous child!

John glanced at Louise; but Louise was gazing fascinated at the baby. Then he looked at Francis who looked back at him with a grin. An *enormous* child! It was really laughable. But the baby was a girl – that was nice. A new little sister, a very small sister . . . perhaps it was because they had just escaped from great danger, while the baby was being born, or because, after that fight, John felt more of a man than ever; but, in any case, he had burning desire to take his little sister in his arms, and protect her against everything for always.

But Father put the baby down again beside its mother.

They went on their knees in a circle round mother and child. The doctor and Father took their hats off; John tore his from Louise's hands, and held the damaged hat over his chest, with folded hands, just like Father, and closed his eyes. His father prayed aloud in a firm, deep voice:

'O Lord, we commend this child to Your care. Her name shall be Indepentia, which means independence. And she shall be baptised in the new land, in the valley of the River Columbia in Oregon. Amen.'

Late in the evening the Sager family's wagon rolled into the camp at Willow Creek Spring. The sun had already set. Boys and girls were sitting on the sandy bank of the creek, dangling their warm feet in the cool water. The splashing they made mingled with their soft, laughing voices. Somewhere a violin was being played, and a young woman was singing to it. A wistful air.

Outside the guide's tent, the leaders of the wagon train were sitting in council in the light of the fire. Henry Sager walked up to them and said something. Heavily they got to their feet, one by one they shook his hand; in the red, restless flickering of the flames their faces were set in serious expressions under their broad-brimmed hats.

Indepentia Sager was the first covered-wagon baby of their caravan. 'The best of luck go with her,' was their wish.

3

The caravan went on.

Accidents happened to the wagons every day. By now the wagon beds and the harness had had so much to endure in that rough country that axles gave way over and over again, poles broke, hoops came off the wheels, and so on. The columns and the individual vehicles became more and more scattered. Only too often did it come to pass that stray groups of wagons did not come rolling into the camping-place until late in the evening, sometimes deep in the night.

The men and women had a hard time of it. But they remained their brave, tenacious selves; after all, they *were* getting on, every day brought them closer to the promised land, for on the average they were still covering twelve to fifteen miles a day.

They travelled south, round Independence Rock, one of the most remarkable sights on their route.

It was a solitary, completely bare mountain of grey granite, towering up from an open plain; at its foot, along its southern side, flowed the lovely Sweetwater river, bordered by an exquisite strip of green grass, which was twenty to thirty feet wide, so that the wagons could easily make their way along it, in single file. The clear water of the river actually tasted sweetish, and was a real treat for the emigrants.

In its grey nakedness, the Rock was most impressive. The names of trappers and explorers had been cut in it, together with the dates.

Henry Sager took his sons John and Francis to look at it. He made them dismount and, hat in hand, read the inscriptions left by those courageous men who, often alone or in small parties, had defied the great dangers of that land in order to chart the way for those who should come after them.

'This rock has been called the Great Register of the Desert,' said Henry Sager. 'Look . . . here it says: "The Oregon Company arrived July 26, 1843." That was last year; and they were the first caravan of pioneers ever to pass through this country. It's a pity Dr Whitman didn't put his own name.'

'Why?' asked Francis.

'Who's Dr Whitman?' asked John.

With a strange glow in his eyes, Henry Sager gazed fixedly towards the west, as he answered, almost absently:

'Marcus Whitman is a medical missionary who works among the Indians at Waiilatpu, in the Columbia valley. He fights for his dream that one day Oregon will become American territory! The British of the Hudson's Bay Company are blocking our way there. They would like it to become British. The Indian tribes, who live from hunting, probably curse both of us. But Whitman foresees that it would be possible for thousands and thousands of Americans to carve out a happy life for themselves in the fertile glens and valleys of Oregon. And that's why, a year ago, by superhuman exertions, he blazed a trail here for the first emigrants. God grant his work will not have been in vain!'

'Is he going to baptise Indepentia?' asked John, sticking closer to homely facts.

'Yes . . . when we reach his mission post, we'll ask him to christen our Indepentia,' said Henry Sager.

With obvious effort, he tore himself away from his vision, and returned to concrete reality.

'We've got to get back to Mother, lads!'

They remounted, with Francis sitting behind his father, and trotted back to the caravan.

That day they made good progress, and before sundown they pitched their camp within sight of the Devil's Gate. While Mother and Louise were roasting thick strips of buffalo meat for the evening meal, above the fire of buffalo droppings, John lay on his stomach in the grass, gazing at that strange 'gate', behind which the sky was still blood-red from the sunset. It was a canyon in a chain of granite mountains – narrow, and with steep sides. Down in the depths, the river flowed through the defile.

'Mother,' John began.

His mother looked at him. In the ruddy glow of the fire she looked less ill and frail than usual.

'Yes, John?'

'May I climb to the top of that, tomorrow?' He pointed to the southern peak of the Devil's Gate.

'Ask your father.'

'But do you think I might? If Willy Ford will go along with me?' John's voice sounded hopeful.

'Oh, if *he* goes with you, I think you might,' his mother replied.

She gave him a big slice of roast meat; the juice was

still dripping from it. John licked his fingers elaborately.

'When we have a house again, you children will have to learn manners again,' said his mother.

John laughed. I'll cross that bridge when I come to it, he thought; it was ridiculously unimportant, anyway. Buffalo meat tasted nice, and that was all that mattered.

Very early next morning, two hours before the caravan was due to move off, John Sager and Willy Ford hit the trail. They had quite a climb ahead of them.

They reached the top of the mountain just as the bugle rang out below to signify that the time for departure had come. They saw the long line of vehicles and animals slowly begin to move.

From the summit on which they stood, the view that met their gaze was so awe-inspiring that it almost took their breath away.

Beneath them was the gaping chasm of the canyon, which, nevertheless, was broader than they had thought — it made their senses reel to look down that sheer wall. Down below, at the bottom, flowed the Sweetwater River. Westward, in the direction in which the caravan was making, a lovely valley stretched, ten to fifteen miles wide, as far as their eyes could see. It looked like an earthly paradise, through which the river wound like a silver ribbon with borders of delicious green on both sides.

'Looks good enough to eat,' said Willy.

'You leave that to the cattle,' said John.

The country was an Eldorado for wild animals: deer,

antelopes, elks, buffalo, mountain goats and mountain sheep, martens, opossums, and skunks, not to mention rabbits. At the foot of the Devil's Gate, running towards the north-west, another such valley stretched to where the Sweetwater River entered the Platte River. Throughout the entire region strange mountains towered up – mountains of granite blocks piled on top of each other, grey, massive, bare, and strange, of which Independence Rock was the strangest of all. And when the lads raised their eyes higher, above and beyond the surrounding plains and valleys, they were met by the circle of mountains. On all sides the horizon was shut off by mountain ridges and peaks; farthest to the west was the snow-capped top of Mount Hood.

For a long time they said nothing. Then Willy suddenly pointed: 'What's that?'

In that long, narrow valley to the north-west there was a dark spot. A big, almost-black patch. It was not forest. It was not stone. It looked as if it was moving. It *was* moving. It was enormous.

'Buffalo!' John shouted. 'It must be buffalo! What a herd – we've never seen anything like it yet! And look – there's another!'

The boys strained their eyes until they nearly popped out of their heads, but they could not distinguish more than black patches. However, their imagination added an immense amount to the little they saw, and that took their breath away.

'We'll go down and report,' said Willy pompously. 'Perhaps we'll be allowed to go along with the hunters tomorrow. After all, *we* discovered them!'

They began to jump down, leaping from boulder to boulder, now and then sliding, in dangerous haste. They picked their way like mountain goats.

That night, buffalo yarns were told round the camp fire. John and Willy were the only boys who were allowed to be there. That was to console them for not having been given permission to go hunting with the rest next day. It was considered too dangerous. Anyone who aspired to go buffalo hunting had to sit extremely firmly in the saddle and be sure of his aim, for otherwise the man would go down instead of the buffalo.

The pioneers had had some experience of that at the start of their journey, long before they reached Fort Laramie.

In the beginning, the first faint shapes of buffalo on a distant ridge had been the signal for a general exodus of everything that called itself a man, could sit in a saddle, and fire a gun. But they had soon found that unpractised hunters on unpractised horses achieved nothing. The horses became jumpy, once in the vicinity of a herd of buffalo, with their rank scent; they began to rear with trembling nostrils, to twist and turn and snort; and, despite a vigorous use of spurs on the part of their riders, they kept a respectful distance from the quarry. And when the herd got irritated and came charging forward, the situation was deadly dangerous. A bull buffalo was a terrible adversary. As a rule, the horse was more sensible then than its reckless rider, and even a wounded buffalo was often enough to make it gallop back to camp, in spite of all that bridle and spurs could do. Only by repeated practice with an experienced hunter was it possible to train a horse for buffalo hunting.

'I once saw buffalo . . . it's a thing I shall never forget,' said a trapper, one of the guide's helpers.

He knocked his pipe out against a stone, filled it again, and lit it. Not until it was going did he continue, his small, screwed-up eyes squinting into the fire.

'I've seen the prairie black with stampeding buffalo, for day after day; as far as you could see. They came in one vast stream, from distant plains to the River Platte, for water, and once they reached the river they plunged into it, and swam across it thousands at a time – there were so many of 'em they not only changed the colour of the water, but its taste as well, it just wasn't drinkable any more. But we had to drink it all the same.'

The weather had remained good ever since they had left Fort Laramie. In fact, it was almost too good to be true. Dismal Jimmies prophesied that it was bound to change soon. Last night, there had been a red rim round the moon. And alas! the pessimists were right.

That night, the wind got up.

At first it was not frightening, but nevertheless the sensible ones among the emigrants went out to tie down their tents and wagon covers extra tightly, and to make sure everything was in order.

The wind grew stronger; it blew quickly; soon it had become a raging storm.

Everything squeaked, creaked, groaned, clattered, slammed, and wailed. The animals outside the corral were scared to death; they stood huddled against each other in dense droves, snorting, restless, lowing from hundreds of throats. Dogs yelped, children cried in the wagons, which shuddered on their wheels. With a tremendous creaking and cracking, as from a clattering clap of thunder, the only tall tree which the camping-ground could boast – a fine old cedar – crashed to the earth.

The families of the emigrants crouched together in their wagons or tents, their hands over their ears, their eyes big with terror.

Then it began to thunder. And it was as if the rolling claps of thunder and the blinding sheets of lightning fanned the storm. In many wagons, people began to pray.

Deafeningly, the tempest raged over the camp. Vehicles were beaten to matchwood, tarpaulins tore loose, tents blew down. On top of that, it began to pour in torrents.

The people of the caravan had never experienced such weather in their lives. Never had they seen such persistent, vivid lightning, never had they heard such a continuous, terrifying rumble of thunder, never had they had to endure such impenetrable sheets of rain. The jets of rain made a sombre, rushing sound, and spouted holes in the ground; everywhere streams arose, which rapidly forced a path to the river. It was as if the world was to come to an end that night; the whole universe trembled and shook. At one moment the immediate vicinity, with beaten-down brushwood and wrecked wagons, was lit up in a blinding white glare by the lightning, and at the next moment everyone and everything had been shut in by an almost palpable, oppressive wall of utter darkness.

Towards sunrise the thunderstorm ceased as suddenly as it had begun. But its cessation hardly brought relief. The destruction was too terrible to be described. Half the wagons had been badly damaged, and some were completely beyond repair. The Sager family's wagon had come off comparatively lightly. Father Sager and John had gone out in good time and done everything they could to make secure what could be secured. And their wagon was a strong, well-built one.

Cathie and Lizzy, who had howled all night without stopping, were sleeping like logs now; Matilda was lying quietly beside them on the blanket, looking up with open eyes at the grey-white canvas of the tilt, which was slowly drying in the warmth of the first rays of the sun. Matilda always reacted quite differently from the others to everything which was 'natural'. It never frightened her. For all her five years she had been braver than nine-year-old Cathie, and less worried than twelve-year-old Louise, who had kept herself under control the whole night, but had listened to the tumult outside with wide eyes in a face drawn with fright and white as chalk, and with her two hands clenched tightly together.

Father Sager left his family behind in the care of Mother and John. He had to go and confer with other responsible men of the expedition, to decide what had to be done. It was obvious that more than half the wagon train would not be able to start that day.

After a conference lasting more than an hour, it was decided that the caravan should split into two. The good, quicker wagons and teams had long been held up and kept back by those which could only go more slowly. Everything that could travel would push on immediately, while the rest would remain behind to carry out the most vital repairs and to recover a little from the ordeal of the night. They were only a few days' journey from Fort Bridger, a recently established, extremely primitive outpost, where Jim Bridger, an old guide and trapper, had fitted up a simple smithy and carpenter's shop to serve the emigrant trains en route. Perhaps the two parties would meet again there; and perhaps not. In any case, they would cover the rest of the journey independently of each other.

Henry Sager remained with the rear group. Not because he would not have been able to travel with the fast party, but because he was the right person to lead and inspire the others, and because no other man of his capacities declared himself willing to stay behind. Moreover, it suited him better, too. His wife had never recovered her strength; she was still languid and weak, she was suffering from dysentery, which grew worse rather than better, and he himself felt less well than he cared to admit. It would be good for them to take things a bit easily. The race was not always to the swift. And his animals would also benefit if he granted them one or two days' more rest.

John was disappointed when he heard of the plan. He would have liked to have gone with the first party. He had already been done out of the buffalo hunt; and, on top of that, came this! But he did not let it spoil his temper. He could take such disappointments. Father had early impressed it on him that he must not let circumstances get him down. And John had been a good pupil. He had as hard a head and as great a capacity for perseverance as his father Henry. But he always resigned himself to the unavoidable, and to decisions whose reasonableness he recognised.

Two days later they set out again. They left the Devil's Gate on their right, and turned south-west. The weather was as fine and bright as it had been for all those weeks before the storm. But no one would ever forget the experience of that night.

John's father, on horseback, led the caravan along in the tracks of the party which had gone on in front two days before. John sat on the driver's seat. He did not like riding in the wagon, but at least he was at the head of the train – in that way, they were not troubled by dust.

Louise did all the housework and looked after the little ones, for Mother lay helpless in the back of the wagon. She was so ill that she could hardly speak a word, and only smiled faintly when Louise or John laid the tiny baby down beside her to be fed.

On the second day of their journey, as the two parallel columns were rolling across the plain at the normal steady, sluggish speed of ox wagons, the drivers and outriders were startled by a strange dull noise from the north, which sounded like the rumble of a very distant storm. But the sky was as clear as could be, in the north and everywhere else.

The rumbling swelled, slowly but steadily; it became a dull droning, constant and regular, growing ever louder and more ominous.

Henry Sager reined in his horse, and scanned through his spyglass the circle of hazy blue mountains bordering the green valley. Behind him, the entire caravan came to a halt.

The dust began to settle. John looked in excitement at his father. He thought of the stories he had heard yesterday, and of what he had seen with his own eyes. There were enormous herds of buffalo in this valley. If . . .

'Stampeding buffalo,' Henry Sager said curtly to the riders beside him.

He passed the spyglass across to one of them. There was a worried look on his face.

'They're coming this way, broadside on to us, at a tremendous pace. With the glass you can already see the front of the herd – yes, that enormous dark-brown mass. We've got to do something. They're charging down on us like a tornado. They've probably been goaded on by hunters, and there'll be no stopping them. They'll dash on in the same direction, and keep going till the end. If they go over us, we might just as well be buried under a stream of lava. We've got to get out of their way.'

He turned in the saddle, and shouted an order behind him:

'Get moving – for all you're worth!'

And he sent his horsemen to the rear, down both sides of the columns, to make sure his order was carried out.

John and the other drivers lashed the oxen with their whips. On, on, on! Now everyone's skin was at stake – those of the animals and those of the people.

Voices shouted, whips cracked and swished, the cattle galloped wildly, hunted forward by the bawling herdsmen; the wagons creaked horribly now that they were being driven at such speed over the uneven ground; horsemen on both sides of the train galloped to and fro to spur the drivers on . . . on, on, on! The last wagons had to be past the danger point before the buffalo herd reached it.

In no time, the caravan was one cloud of dust; no driver could see beyond the wall of dust enclosing him and his oxen. Everyone breathed dust. Everyone bit dust. The animals ran blindly behind each other, led by smell and sound. On, on, on!

But even the din made by the caravan was drowned by that tremendous thundering, coming nearer and nearer.

On, on, on!

'We shan't make it,' one of the foremost horsemen panted.

Up in front, they were not hindered by the dust, and they could see the sea of humped brown backs rolling terrifyingly closer.

'We shan't make it,' he said again, his voice breaking with fear.

Henry Sager, who had been mute since giving that last order, looked at him darkly.

'*We* shall, but the last ones won't. Get to the back, and collect all the mounted men on the north side of our tail. Have all the cattle driven to the south side, behind the wagons. I'll follow you in a minute. We've got to keep going like this for a while.'

The man turned his horse about and galloped off. Father Sager looked behind him. He tried to pierce the eddying clouds of dust with his eyes, but he could not see the foremost vehicles, he could only hear the snorting and the thundering hooves of the oxen behind him.

'Drive as hard as you can, John!' he shouted. 'Make the animals give all they've got. The others'll follow you all right!'

The oxen snorted and panted, the horses began to whinny restlessly. The long whips cracked without ceasing.

Once again, Henry Sager estimated the distance still separating them from the approaching horde of buffalo. It was high time for the last desperate measures.

He turned his horse, drove his spurs into its sides and, bending down over its neck, clenched his teeth and rode straight into the cloud of dust. In the rear he found forty or so mounted men, who were riding on the north side of the caravan, between the wagons and the threatening danger.

'Dismount!' Sager roared. 'Set light to the grass and all the bushes you can find! Look alive!'

But he need not have said those last words.

In less than no time a wall of flames blazed up. The men withdrew behind and to either side of it.

The buffalo were close now; the dull rumble of thousands upon thousands of trampling hooves mingled with the bellowing of thousands of throats. The ground trembled and shook with their wild galloping. They were running against the wind. The stinging smoke blew towards them. They saw the flames. But like mad creatures they still charged straight towards them. The leaders were driven forward by all that ran behind.

To anyone who could have seen it, the whole northern part of the plain would have looked like one vast moving wave or stream. It was as if the mountains on the horizon were ceaselessly vomiting out a black, undulating mass, under which all unevennesses in the ground disappeared.

It seemed as if the earth would burst asunder from those thundering hooves. Men shouted, horses tore violently at their bridles and whinnied with terror. Dogs howled and barked. The hairy humps of the buffalo could now be seen, and in their shaggy heads the smouldering points of their eyes, which caught the sun.

Henry Sager sat as if turned to stone. His knees gripped his horse convulsively. He knew his own family was safe; but these last wagons, with their precious cargo of human lives, had also been entrusted to his care.

And now he gave his last command.

'Shoot! Shoot off all the rifles and pistols, right

through the flames, and here at the northern point of the fire. They've got to wheel south-east!'

Shouting, the men passed his order on. For a moment, all other sounds seemed drowned in one ear-splitting report. Gun after gun was shot off at random. Bang, bang, bang!

It was now or never. If fire, smoke, and shooting, all together, were of no avail, they were lost. The suspense was well-nigh unbearable. No one breathed.

But it worked!

The foremost buffalo could not stop – the force behind them was too tremendous; if they had tried to stop, they would have been trampled under foot and pulverised. But they did begin to turn. They swung off to the left, to the south-east. Just where the wall of fire and smoke covered the tail end of the rearguard, the extreme right flank of the herd rolled by. The ground droned loudly for a second, the air throbbed with the snorting bellowing, but the danger was past. The animals streamed by as if crazed, blind and deaf, wild and terrible because of their sheer mass; but they no longer inspired fear. With hoarse throats the men shouted a hurrah. Tears were running down the cheeks of some of them.

The train came to a standstill. The oxen were dead beat. From all the wagons, men, women and children poured out to see the spectacle. A dozen buffalo lay dead and partly crushed beside the ceaselessly onward-flowing, dark-brown, hairy mass. In a sea of backs the herd rolled on; in thousands upon thousands it rolled on.

John came riding up, slowly, his eyes staring fixedly at the incredible sight. He had Francis sitting behind, and little Matilda was on the saddle in front of him. Like all the others, he was grey with dust, and the sweat was running in streams down his temples.

His face, striped with dirt, broke into a smile, when Matilda turned her little head, looked up at him, and said: 'What a lot, John, eh?'

It was decided that the emigrants would go no farther that day. An hour later, while the buffalo were still streaming past, the wagons were driven into a circle. The corral was formed. The oxen were watered at a creek, and there was grass and to spare for them to the west of the buffalo stampede.

At last, when the sun's beams were slanting from the west, and the bushes were casting long shadows, the stream began to come to an end. And within quite a short time not a single buffalo was to be seen with the naked eye. The wind blew the rank stench of their trail away from the camp. Where the wild horde had passed, the plain, once so green, had been churned up until it was completely black. The fire had died out on the edge of that desert.

That night, two things happened in the Sager family.

When the last red light of the sun lit up the tops of the western hills, Louise Sager sought in vain for little Matilda, who had to go to bed. It was John who finally found her. In spite of strict orders to the contrary, she had left the corral and was lying drowsily, with tears on her cheeks, against the back of a dead young buffalo cow, whose head she was languidly stroking. When John picked her up, he checked the scolding he had been going to give her, for she looked at him with a deeply sad expression on her face and said:

'It's got such lovely shining eyes, and now p'raps they'll never live any more.'

Swiftly he carried Matilda to the corral and put her in their wagon.

He arrived just in time to see his father clutch at his stomach, retch, and sink to his knees with a face as white as chalk.

With the help of a neighbour, Louise and John laid him beside Mother in the wagon. Mother was feeding Indepentia. John looked tenderly at the little black head against Mother's white shoulder in the dusk of the canvas tilt. He felt quite particularly fond of that little sister of his.

Father opened his eyes; he gave Mother a sidelong glance, which said: now the pair of us are lying here sick. But she smiled, as if to say: we'll be better by and by.

Beads of sweat broke out on Father's forehead.

'Now *you'll* have to look after the family, John,' he said hoarsely; and those words sent a shiver down John's spine.

Surely, Father was only a bit unwell? He only meant that John would have to care for the family as long as the illness lasted.

The boy nodded reassuringly.

'And Francis is here, too, Father,' he said.

Francis, who had already been lying rolled in his blanket, but had crept up on his knees again in order to be able to see everything as well as possible, blushed a rosy red with pleasure at John's words. Fortunately, no one could see that he was blushing. Very content, he lay down once more.

4

In the evening of a hot day early in July Kit Carson, one of the most famous trappers of the time, came across a small emigrants' camp between Fort Bridger and the Sublette Cutoff. Only one wagon was standing there; two horses and a number of cows were trying to find food between the stones and sagebrush.

Carson rode up at a gallop, leapt from his horse, and ordered a boy who came towards him to put out the fire.

It was a lad with hair bleached almost white by the sun and a face full of freckles. He was wearing a long red flannel shirt that came down to his knees. In his leather belt he had stuck two knives and a powder horn. The belt sagged crookedly round his narrow boy's hips with the weight of a heavy pistol in a holster. His eyes were bright and intelligent.

Without hesitation he did as Carson told him.

He ran to the wagon, brought out a spade, and threw earth over the fire of buffalo droppings. Not until he had finished did he look up and ask: 'Why do I have to do this?'

The strange man looked at him. Then he turned his eyes to the row of children's faces staring from the wagon. It was late, and they ought really to have been asleep. The big boy glanced round at them and frowned. Then he laughed shyly, and said, awkwardly pointing:

'That's my brother and sisters.'

'Oh, is that so?' said Carson, with a sick feeling in his stomach.

Those children were in danger. Indians were usually above killing children, but the grown-ups who must surely also be there ran every risk of being butchered. And if that happened, what would become of the kids? And how in the world did this one wagon come to be standing there, all on its own, in the middle of the wilderness?

'Why did I have to put out the fire?' John Sager asked again.

'Because there's a party of Sioux Indians on the warpath, that's why. They mustn't spy that smoke,' Carson replied. It was best to tell the truth. 'Where's your father?'

'Father and Mother are both lying ill in the wagon.'

'How do you come to be alone here like this?' asked the trapper.

'The other wagons are two days' journey in front of us,' the boy answered. 'We couldn't get any farther. I had to repair one of the wagon axles first. But it's all right now. Father told me exactly what I had to do.'

'Just take me inside there, will you? I'd like to see your father.'

They walked up to the wagon. The children's faces in the white frame of the cover receded. With one foot already in the wagon, Carson turned towards the boy; he looked down at his sturdy, freckled face and asked:

'What's your name?'

'Sager,' said John. 'Father's name is Henry, and I am John Sager.'

'Hm,' said the trapper, but what he thought was: mighty cute lad, that.

It was dark in the wagon. Carson felt and heard children's bodies creeping and squirming round him; and he heard the sound of breath being drawn in gasps somewhere at the back. He took his tinderbox out of his pocket and struck a light.

'I'm never allowed to do that in the wagon now Father's ill,' said John. 'Risk of fire,' he added dryly.

Carson blew the flame out. He smiled to himself in the dark.

'Your eyes'll get used to the darkness,' the boy's voice went on, 'if you'll only wait a little. Father's lying in the back. Please don't tread on Indepentia's basket, that's on the left.'

'Indepentia?' growled Carson.

'Our baby,' John explained, with a note of pride in his voice.

Heaven above, a baby in this company, too!

His eyes did adjust themselves to the darkness. It was not long before he could make out two figures lying stretched out on a drab tarpaulin.

'That's Father and Mother,' John whispered. 'They sleep a lot. And Father's delirious sometimes. But Louise says that's the way to get better.'

Carson bent down and scrutinised the wasted white faces of the man and woman as well as he could.

'What have you got in the way of food?' he asked John in a whisper.

'The day before yesterday I shot an antelope and three rabbits, and we're still living on them. But Father and Mother can't keep any meat down. They drink water. But our water's nearly gone, and we're nowhere near any spring or river here. It's not such a good camping-place,' he ended shamefacedly.

Carson shook the man's shoulder. But he did not wake up. His eyes flickered half-open for a moment, then closed again.

'Come outside,' Carson ordered John suddenly, under his breath. He found it difficult to breathe there; if it came to that, the air in the wagon was not fresh, to say the least of it.

He could not help them. He had to go on. The trappers' camp at Green River Rendezvous had to be warned that the Sioux were on their way with anything but friendly intentions. He could not stay with the children even for that one night. But the lad beside him appeared to be very much of a man. If they could only see to it that they left this place like greased lightning and caught up with the others. . . .

'Listen, John,' he said, laying a hand on the boy's shoulder. He noticed how muscular that shoulder and arm were. 'You harness your oxen to your wagon, and drive as fast as you can, day and night, without stopping, until you come up with the rest of the troop. Do you understand? Day and night, without stopping. If you're right about them being two days' journey ahead, you'll have joined up with them by tomorrow night. Don't spare either yourself or the animals.'

With the last words he leapt back into the saddle

with a flourish. He looked piercingly at the boy, as if to convince him of the seriousness of the situation by the force of his eyes alone. He could not have said how wretched he felt at having to leave those children behind like that.

'When your father wakes up, tell him he's got a good son,' he called over his shoulder, after he had turned his horse round and jabbed his spurs into the animal's side. He thundered off, while John stood looking after him flabbergasted.

Deep in thought, John went and yoked the oxen. Poor brutes, they had a hard haul before them. And he would not be gentle with them – any more than he would be gentle with himself, or with any of the others.

It was completely breathless animals and an exhausted young driver which, after a journey of two nights and two days, approached the emigrants' camp near Soda Springs on Bear River as night was falling. Only a small corral stood there; John counted a mere twelve wagons. Evidently the caravan had disintegrated even more, and the others were still farther ahead.

He saw at once that it was a splendid camping-place.

The water of the river murmured enticingly, the several hundred head of cattle grazed greedily on the luxuriant green grass, and the hills round about were covered with the most beautiful fir and cedar trees, which shone like silver in the late night. A spring spouted deliciously fresh water, and a gigantic mountain of red-brown, fantastically shaped stones, which looked as if they had been vomited forth as glowing cinders by a volcano, made the spot appear even wilder and more beautiful than it was.

John's eyes, which, during the journey, he had had a job to keep from closing, suddenly opened wide to take in the wondrous sights before them. But it was not only the beauty around him which gave him such a funny feeling inside. It was all such a relief . . . that they were among human beings again – that there was someone there who might be able to help Father and Mother and Indepentia – that, at last, he would be able to sleep.

On the edge of the camp he reined his oxen in, and asked whether perhaps the doctor was with this troop, or, if not, whether there was a woman there who knew anything about nursing sick people.

'Ha, John Sager!' someone cried, and Willy Ford's father came running up. He started at the sight of the boy's utterly weary face.

'Is the doctor here?' John repeated his question impatiently.

'Yes – that's to say, if you mean the vet . . .'

John nodded. He was too tired to say one word more than was necessary.

'Bring him here. Please. Please. Father and Mother are very ill. For two days now, Mother's been too ill to feed the baby, and I can't get her to take anything else. We've tried to feed her on sugar and water and cow's milk.'

Father Ford went trotting off to fetch the doctor.

John looked thankfully after him. He felt too exhausted to go a step farther himself. He remained sitting on the driver's seat, his elbows on his knees, and his head in his hands.

His drowsy eyelids were beginning to droop again. They were so strangely heavy, and all the sounds he heard were becoming so queer – as if they came from a great distance off. He felt Francis come and sit beside him. Louise was busy in the back of the wagon. She was trying to soothe Indepentia, who was crying pitifully. Yesterday she had screamed loudly all day, but evidently she no longer had strength left for that. 'Quiet now, quiet now,' he heard Louise saying, as if she was very far away from him. 'Quiet now, quiet now . . .'

The sound of men's voices startled him into wakefulness. There came Ford and Johnston and Michael O'Connell and Red Pete. Others were following. The doctor was walking in front. With his long legs, he jumped up beside John and into the wagon. John wanted to follow him, but the doctor sent him away.

He sent the children out of the wagon. In the twinkling of an eye all those red shirts were sitting beside each other in a row in the grass, which was beginning to grow damp from the night mist. Above the river a bluish vapour hung, and the tops of the encircling mountains glowed red in the sunset. It had been a hot day. No one said a word; all waited in suspense.

It did not last long. The doctor came out. He did not

look at John and the other children. And it was with
difficulty that he spoke when he said to the waiting
crowd:

'They're dead – both of them, Henry Sager and his
wife.'

'It's not true, it's a lie!' John screamed.

He leapt at the doctor and repeated his words,
screaming, shouting, crying. His throat felt as if a hand
were round it, strangling him; he *had* to scream, to get
rid of that pain, that pain in his throat and in his chest:

'It isn't true, it isn't true!'

The doctor seized his hands, but he tore loose
and tried to climb into the wagon. Two or three
compassionate hands pulled him back.

Then he threw himself on the ground, on his
stomach; he buried his head in the cool, moist grass, he
bit it, to prevent himself from bursting out crying
again.

Father and Mother dead – dead, dead, dead: Father,
whom he could not do without, and Mother, dear,
dear Mother, with her gentle face, and dark, deep
eyes – Mother's mouth, Mother's shoulder with
Indepentia's little head on it!

That child! What was to become of that tiny child?
It was as though a mountain came rolling over John, a
burden so heavy, so impossible to lift, so indescribably
oppressive, that he felt as if he was suffocating.

A smothered sob was forced up from his throat. It
hurt; it hurt more than he could bear. He tried to lie
quite still, but his shoulders began to shake, his whole
body trembled, something gave way in his throat, and

the sobs came jerkily, shudderingly, one after the other.

'Father and Mother . . .' he cried, 'Father and Mother. . . .'

Suddenly he felt a hot little hand on the back of his neck.

Without looking he knew it was Matilda. Little Matilda. That was how she had sat beside the dead buffalo cow. He remembered it so clearly – it was as though he still saw her sitting there. Comforting, caressing – and she was only five years old. And he was nearly fourteen.

He had to do the comforting. It was his duty to look after the others, to help them. How were they now? He did not dare to look up yet. For a brief while longer he let that little hand do its soothing work. There was something singularly calming about it. Little Matilda . . . touched, he looked up at last, and saw her peaked, solemn child's face. It was the shape of a heart; he had never seen that so clearly as now. With the parting down the middle of her hair, above her broad forehead. And the small pointed chin below her triangular mouth. She looked at him, and her hand slid caressingly down the arm with which he was now leaning on the ground.

'John, do, do stop crying,' she said. 'If you cry *I* can't cry, and I want to cry, because everyone else is crying.'

In spite of everything. John had to smile. She had hit the nail so exactly on the head. She was only five years old, she had a right to cry. He hadn't. He was the eldest. He had to be a support for the children.

He sat up, and stretched out his hand. She laid her

cheek in the hollow of it, and then she began to do what she had meant to do. She wept. Big, quiet tears.

Cathie and Lizzy were both crying in long, screaming sobs. Cathie because she realised that Father and Mother really never would wake up any more, ever; and Lizzy because everyone else was crying, and everything was so nasty and strange. Two women took the little girls away with them.

Up till then, Louise and Francis had been sitting quietly weeping side by side. Francis had angrily shaken the pitying hand of Mrs Ford from his shoulder. Now they got up, and both walked with dragging feet and tears running down their cheeks to John and Matilda. They sat down beside them.

No one ventured to disturb the children for the time being.

As quietly as possible two women and a man climbed into the wagon to prepare the dead couple for burial. After brief consultation, it had been decided to bury them that same evening. That would make it possible for the children to sleep in their own wagon for the night. Moreover, the caravan had to be on its way again early the following morning.

John looked sombrely on when Mrs Ford went off with Indepentia in her arms, wrapped in Mother's purple Sunday shawl – just as on that first day. The baby had stopped crying now; she must have fallen asleep.

John himself also fell asleep . . . at last. He lay in the grass, and Francis and Louise combined efforts and rolled him up in a blanket. He did not wake up.

The caravan travelled on.

By now, it was but a small column of ox wagons which made its way across the superb wild mountain country en route for Fort Hall, a British fur traders' post. Before them, two columns had already turned off to the south-west – California was more attractive to settlers than Oregon, where obstruction from the British was to be expected. But in both cases it was necessary to travel through difficult mountain country.

John sat on the driver's bench, Louise sat beside him. They were Father and Mother now. They had not said one word about it, but they both felt it that way. Francis and the others accepted John's authority.

Francis rode on horseback behind the cattle.

'Tough little devil,' said the other herdsmen, approvingly.

They had respect for those Sager children.

On the evening of the second day – they were due to reach Fort Hall on the morrow – John was called before the small council of representatives which ruled all such wagon trains. In this council was vested the legislative and executive power to which everyone had to submit. Admittedly, anyone could speak and plead his cause before this assembly if necessary; but there was no appeal against the decisions it took. You had to accept them. That was an unwritten law.

'Scrub your ears well before you go, John,' Louise admonished him.

She gave him a clean handkerchief, and before he

left the wagon she solemnly handed him Father's hat. She considered that John had a right to wear that now. In silence he settled the far too big hat down on his clean ears.

In silence he betook himself to the council, which was sitting in a semicircle in front of a big camp fire. Smoking, and also silent. John felt that danger threatened him in some way, and he was resolved to stand firm.

The oldest of the men motioned to John to sit down on the ground along with them. Then he cleared his throat, taking longer to do it than was necessary, and began:

'We may as well go straight to the point, lad – it's no good beating about the bush. You children can't stay together. A household made up of kids, all by themselves in one wagon, runs too great risks. So we've divided you among three families. You and Lizzy are to go in with the O'Connells, Louise and Matilda along with the Mullers, Francis and Cathie are coming with me, Indepentia will stay with Mrs Ford. That's the best way of arranging it. I hope you agree.'

It was all John could do to let him finish. He realised that a lot depended now on his keeping calm. He had to be as much like Father as possible. They had to have confidence in him. His fingernails were pressed tightly into the palms of his hands. He knew that Father and Mother would think it terrible if they did not stay together, not to speak of what he thought about it himself – and the others. . . .

'Sir,' said John – he didn't know how else to begin –

'I quite realise that you think it's best that way. If I was you, I might think so myself. But if I did, it would be because I didn't know the children well enough. I mean' – he laughed shyly – 'you don't really know us so terribly well. You don't know how good Louise is at washing and baking bread and – and all sorts of things. She's had to do them long enough already for Mother. And Francis and Cathie can look after our cattle very well. Cathie has to be taken firmly in hand, sometimes, that's all – she always has tummy-ache if she's got to do something; but we're strict with her, and we can't complain. I can handle the oxen and horses, and I can shoot and hunt, too, perhaps better than you think, because Father always said, "You shoot mighty well, John, for a boy of your age." If it comes to that . . . I'm not all that young either, am I? I shall be fourteen next month.'

He stopped and glanced round the circle of men.

They sat looking kindly at him, but he could not see that clearly in the unsteady flickering of the flames. The lad was remarkably like his father, they thought – in the slow, judicious way in which he spoke, and also in his gestures, which had a certain power of conviction. John Sager inspired confidence. That again was exactly what his father had always done. And he wasn't stupid, either, for he cunningly added:

'I think Lizzy and Cathie would be *very* troublesome if they were to go to other people. That would be no joke for anybody . . . and we want Indepentia back,' he ended resolutely, carrying the war into the enemy's camp, and thus employing the best tactics without knowing it.

The men looked at each other, pushed their hats to the back of their heads, scratched behind their ears, sucked at their pipes – in short, they pondered deeply. Young John Sager was someone to be reckoned with.

'We'll let you try to stay together,' was the decision. 'We'll see how things go. But the baby stays with Mrs Ford.'

5

In south-east Idaho there is an area where the Snake River has now been dammed up at the American Falls, a tremendous cataract feeding one of the biggest electric power stations in America. A vast sheet of water covers what was once barren wilderness. And there, a hundred years ago, lay Fort Hall.

It was a small, roughly built, stone fort, where a few employees of the Hudson's Bay Company traded in furs with the Indians, completely cut off from the rest of the world. The Indians brought hides and beaver skins to them; in exchange, the white men gave them tobacco, powder, lead, rifles, mirrors, beads, splendidly decorated cast-off army uniforms for their chiefs, and, later, whisky. Fortunes were amassed in fur trading – all the top hats in the Old and the New World were made from the silky beaver skins.

About half-way through July, in the year 1844, the little caravan of American emigrants with which the Sager children were travelling arrived at that British outpost. They were hospitably received there; they were treated to good food and even to wine and tobacco; but when their future plans came up for discussion, the factor shook his head.

The men were sitting in the shade of a penthouse in the fort's inner courtyard, which was overgrown with short grass. Two Indian women were serving them with strips of roast buffalo meat, tender steaks of horseflesh, and Indian 'honey balls', in which whole legs, wings and heads of grasshoppers were to be found. Glasses were clinked and healths were drunk, but nevertheless the atmosphere was not cheerful. As good British subjects and loyal employees of the Hudson's Bay Company, the factor and his men were hard at work trying to dissuade the emigrants from trekking on to Oregon.

The emigrants, tired out and already thoroughly discouraged by the manifold adversities that had come their way, did not know that those warnings were addressed to anyone and everyone who appeared there with a covered wagon and intended to go and settle in Oregon. For the men of the Hudson's Bay Company, Oregon had to remain a fur-trapping area, and perhaps, in the future, become British territory. Hence, American settlers were unwelcome. They reduced the chances of the British; for, once a sufficient number of American subjects lived there, the American Government would no doubt take the necessary steps to annex the no man's land of Oregon.

'You're taking wagons over the mountains to the Columbia valley?' asked the factor, as if he could not believe his ears. 'What's got into you men? Don't you people know *anything*? Haven't you any idea of the kind of wilderness you'll land up in there?'

'Maybe . . . but Dr Whitman got through with a wagon train last year, didn't he?' the obstinate Irishman O'Connell retorted.

'Whitman? I take my hat off to him! I've never met a man to touch that one! But not everybody can do what he did! And it was lunacy, even when *he* did it. And what was the price he had to pay, in human lives, in cattle, horses, and equipment? You don't know *that*!'

'But at any rate there's a trail now which we'll be able to follow, more or less,' O'Connell persisted. 'That makes a lot of difference.'

'A trail? You show it me! What there was in the way of a trail has been swallowed up by the wilderness again, by snowstorms, sandstorms, avalanches, the tracks of wild animals, and Indians running across it – man, what *are* you thinking of?'

'I'm thinking of trying it!'

'If you go too far to the north, you'll get lost in a region of deep chasms, ravines, towering mountain peaks, impassable passes. But you can't go too far to the south, either, 'cos if you do you'll find no water. You've got to cross rivers; you've even got to cross the Snake twice, and no party's ever succeeded in doing it *once* without losing people and cattle, because the current's so tremendously strong. But when you've done that don't think you've had the lot! Before you even reach the Boisé River, you have to pass through an area where three or four Indian tribes have banded together to bar the way to white men. Quite rightly, they're beginning to get anxious about their precious hunting grounds. And then, if you manage to keep out of the hands of those savages, you've an even worse enemy to face: hunger. Because it's such a darned long way that winter will have fallen before you've made the Cascade Mountains.

'On the other hand . . . if you go to California, to the south-west, the route's considerably shorter. And easier.'

The factor fell silent. That was a long speech, for him; but it was not a speech he was delivering for the first time. And, just as on the previous occasions, his words would bear fruit.

That night, a serious conference took place round the camp fire just outside the fort. The meeting did not last long, for agreement was soon reached. They would follow the advice of the British factor. The caravan would turn off south to California, as those which had passed through there before had done, according to the factor.

John, who was now allowed to be present at the gatherings of the caravan council, even though he was not allowed to say anything, sat chafing with indignation. They had got right as far as here, far more than half-way, at the cost of many sacrifices and great exertions; they had lost people, cattle, wagons, and goods; and were they going to give up *now*? If so, why all those sacrifices?

Out of his grief for the loss of his father and mother, a burning, urgent desire had grown in him. For as long as he could remember it had been his father's dream to possess a big farm in the valley of the Columbia River, in order thus to do his bit to ensure that Oregon should become American soil. John wanted to carry out his father's wish – he wanted to reach that splendid Land of Promise, he did *not* want the plan to be given up now that they had come so far. If the others wouldn't go with him, he would go alone! He and his sisters and brother. *They would get there. The Sagers would get to Oregon.*

While the voices of the men buzzed around him, he solemnly took that resolve, in silence. Staring into the camp fire with unseeing eyes, he pondered plans.

Until someone tapped him on the shoulder. He was on cattle-guard duty for the first half of the night. He went to fetch his gun.

Early next morning he discussed his scheme with Louise and Francis. Francis agreed immediately. Louise looked concerned, but said she was willing, all the same. 'It will be very difficult, though, John.'

'Yes, it'll be very difficult, but it'll come off,' said John, and clamped his teeth round the stem of Father's pipe, in which he smoked kinnickinick, the ground-up bark of the red willow.

The entire day was occupied in secret preparations. They wanted to leave that same night; every day was precious. They had no time to lose. It went without saying that no one must know they were going, otherwise they would be stopped.

They would leave the wagon behind. John chose their strongest ox, and their most robust young cow, to carry stores, weapons, blankets, and tent. They did not dare take the two horses with them, for fear of the Indians, who would steal horses as soon as look at them. Horses would be a bait for them. Possession of a horse was everything to an Indian. And not every Indian had one.

Louise piled in a corner of the wagon all the articles she thought might be of use on the way. Flour and the last of their sugar, salt bacon, dried and minced buffalo meat, a kettle and a pan, blankets and canvas, towels, the Bible, and sewing materials. John laid the rifles on the pile, with everything that went with them, ramrods, powder, lead, percussion caps; and the water skins. He hung Father's big tinderbox firmly on his belt, and Father's hunting knife too. His own he gave to Francis.

They did everything in an atmosphere of great tension; they hardly said a word, or looked at each other.

They felt they were about to undertake something risky, whose outcome was not certain. But they would not admit it to each other.

At last there remained only two, very important, things to be done. They had to fetch Indepentia, and John wanted to get hold of a dog.

'Louise,' said John, 'give me Father's last tobacco and Mother's silver locket. There are Indians at the fort, and one of them goes around with a very nice wolf dog.'

'D'you mean to say you want to barter Mother's locket for a dog?' asked Louise, sharply. It was the first time she had come near to losing her temper; but she was disappointed in John for wanting to get rid of Mother's one and only piece of jewellery. The old locket on the little silver chain, which she had always worn round her neck.

'How do you think *I* feel about it?' John retorted

roughly. It was because he felt so bad about it himself that he grew angry. Louise ought to realise that he wasn't doing it for fun. It was for the safety of all of them that he was having to do it. He could not stand on guard every night. And the dog would come in useful in hunting, too.

Louise said nothing. She still could not see the importance of having a dog.

'Do you want the Indians to take us by surprise, or one of the children to be eaten by wolves or by a grizzly bear?' John asked impatiently. 'Come on, give it up!'

Still without saying a word, Louise took the locket out of the little bag of needles and thread which she had laid ready to be taken with them. She picked its little cover open with her fingernail, and took the miniature portraits out of it: a black silhouette of Father as a young man, with a fierce moustache whipped up high at the ends, and a drawing of John as a tiny boy, wearing a big straw hat with a broad white ribbon round it. Then she shut the locket again and gave it to him. She gulped, and said: 'I understand – but it makes me feel so bad, that's all.'

John stowed it in his pocket. Suddenly he had the greatest difficulty in keeping back his tears. And nevertheless he was glad. He was glad that Louise and he found the same things nasty and hard, and the same things good and pleasant. He would dearly have liked to have thrown his arms round her neck; but you didn't do that sort of thing, as a man . . . now he came to think of it, it was *such* a long time since he had given anyone a kiss. It seemed as if Mother had been dead for ages, and yet it had only happened last week.

He turned his back on her with a jerk.

'I think I'll go and fetch Indepentia first. I can see about the dog presently,' he said brusquely.

Indepentia, at any rate, was something a man could hold in his arms without losing his self-respect – of a sudden he was seized with an almost unbearable longing to press his cheek against her warm, soft, little head. And it was comforting to think that she would never give him away if he did.

He began to run. Walton's wagon, in which the Fords were living, was right opposite theirs in the corral.

'Mrs Ford, may we have Indepentia, just for this evening?' he began. 'We haven't had her with us for so long. And we'll look after her well.'

Mrs Ford looked at him doubtfully.

'Oh, *please*,' John pleaded, 'if you'll only let us have her this evening, and perhaps for tonight too, we'll give you a bit of sugar. Please, please, Mrs Ford – we can look after her very well – after all, she drinks cow's milk now, and she's *so* good. It won't do her any harm. Please. We'll let you have two cupfuls of sugar.'

He felt a wretched fraud. But he salved his conscience by telling himself that Indepentia herself would certainly sooner be with them than with Mrs Ford. And, when all was said and done – Indepentia *was* theirs.

Mrs Ford was terribly tempted by that sugar. But Indepentia Sager had been entrusted to her care; and

suppose anything should happen to her . . .! But there
. . . the Sagers were such good, serious, dependable
children – all right, then! And Indepentia wasn't the
sort of baby to get easily hurt.

'You'll be sure to take good care of her, won't you
John? And remember, lad, don't give her pure milk, put
a dash of warm water in it.'

'Yes, Mrs Ford.'

How excited the boy sounded. And how eagerly he
stretched out his arms for his baby sister. She was no
more than a little bundle, in his mother's shawl. That
lock of black hair only just stuck out of it.

John repressed his grin of delight until he was out of
sight of Mrs Ford. Then he ventured to bow his face
for a moment, and put his cheek against Indepentia's
warm baby head.

'Indepentia,' he whispered, 'you're going to
Oregon. Along with us. And you'll grow up in a
lovely valley among flowers and bean boles and
wheat and maize and – and oranges.' But actually he
did not know for certain whether oranges could
grow in Oregon. Oh well, they would find that out
when they arrived.

'I've got her!' he said, when he reached their
own wagon, and lifted her up and put her into the
outstretched arms of Louise, who bent down to
receive her from where she had been standing waiting.
Inside, Indepentia was laid down in her old place.

'Now I'm going for the dog!' John cried
exuberantly, and was off in a flash.

He returned with a prize. A real wolf dog, perhaps

eighteen months old. On his way back from the fort he had picked up Francis, whom he had sent out to spy out the land early that morning.

'At first the Indian wouldn't do it, of course. But I'd kept back half the tobacco, and when I put that along with the rest, it was all right. I didn't even show him the locket,' he said, with a sidelong look at Louise.

He was holding the dog on a leash. The animal was not accustomed to that, and when John tried to stroke his head he growled and showed his teeth.

Louise looked anxious.

'Then I'm afraid you've let yourself be swindled,' she said.

John jerked his shoulder, as if to say: come off it! People don't swindle me so easily.

But Francis said shrewdly:

'I guess that Indian thinks the dog will find its way back to him of its own accord. And then he'll have both tobacco and dog.'

John shook his head.

'We'll tie him up good and tight. And tonight, when we go, he'll run on the leash.'

'He'll bolt off anyway when we're two days' journey farther,' Francis prophesied.

'I'll shoot a deer and give him good meat to eat,' said John. All the same, he was beginning to get a little afraid that his younger brother might turn out to be right. The bargain had been very easily made. And Indians were crafty.

'As if that Indian didn't give him any meat!' Francis scoffed.

'We'll see,' John said abruptly. He had suddenly caught sight of Matilda walking towards them. He wanted her to help him. She became close chums with every animal she came across.

She was toiling along, hugging to her little round stomach a much too heavy pot of batter belonging to a neighbour. But no sooner did she see John, with the dog beside him, than she was there in a flash. The pot of batter was planked down in the grass, and had been lapped up in less than no time by another dog, which came shooting forward. Mrs O'Connell threw up her arms and screamed, but by then it was already too late.

Matilda stood right in front of John's dog and looked at him in a friendly fashion. She gently laid her hand on his head; he permitted the liberty. Then she dropped down on her knees in front of him, and put an arm round his neck. The animal sat down. They remained sitting beside each other like that for quite a while.

John gave the leash to Matilda.

'You take him to the wagon,' he said.

'What's his name?' asked Matilda.

'The Indian called him Shongsasha,' John replied. 'I thought we might call him Oscar.'

'Oscar,' Matilda whispered very, very softly in the dog's ear. 'Oscar.'

'Go on, take him to the wagon,' John repeated.

'Right-oh.'

She got up, put her little hand on the dog's head, and walked to the wagon.

'Come on, Oscar,' she said.

The dog went along with her, the leash dragging behind him in the grass.

That night, Matilda slept under the wagon with the dog beside her.

More than an hour before the first rays of the sun were due to appear above the hills, the great adventure began.

The previous evening, John had told the younger children all about it, and had impressed them with the necessity of not making a sound when they left. Francis had reconnoitred the route. First they would have to go some distance to the south-east; then over a patch of marshy land above rocky subsoil – there, all tracks were washed away at once; and then they would have to go round behind a hill, to reach the right trail, in a north-westerly direction.

In the wagon they were abandoning, John left a note:

I am on my way back to the United States with my brother and sisters. If we hurry, we shall still be able to go along with Kit Carson from Green River Rendezvous.

JOHN SAGER

He could not have thought of a better way of putting the others off the scent. The children's tracks led eastwards, and the note said why. If anyone were to ride after them, they would not be found anyway.

John had so arranged matters as to be on cattle-guard duty for part of the night. He spent that time in loading the ox and cow with the packsaddles and leather saddle-bags from the horses, behind a clump of tall peppermint shrubs a short distance away from the camp.

He succeeded better than he had expected in getting everything roped securely round their awkwardly shaped bodies. On the way he intended to make *traineaux*, the things he had seen the Indians using at Fort Laramie – big wicker baskets, suspended behind the animal between poles. But for the time being they would have to get along like this. It was fortunate that the beasts were so docile.

Before he was due to be relieved, he took the others a short way along their road.

He carried Lizzy on his back and Indepentia, warmly wrapped up, in his arms. She never cried in John's arms, and besides he was afraid that, in the darkness, Louise might trip over unevennesses in the rough ground. Francis carried one rifle over his shoulder, and another in his left hand; with his right he led the ox by the halter. Louise led the cow, holding Matilda by the hand, and Matilda, in her turn, held tightly on to Cathie. Oscar the dog walked close at Matilda's heels. His muzzle came up to her shoulder.

They did not say a word, and walked as quietly as possible through the night, which was growing lighter.

The older children were labouring under violent

tension; it was as if everything in them vibrated. And every sound made them jump. A dog barked; farther away an ox lowed and another answered; from the camp came the noise of a clanking chain, another dog began to bark – with their hearts in their mouths they crept on. The moon was low in the sky, and the stars were beginning to pale. Soon the sun would rise.

If only they could get behind that hill, out of sight of the camp!

Francis was walking in front now. They were passing through the bog; boots and hooves were sucked tightly into the mud, and made a soft smacking sound when they were pulled out. Smooth brown water snakes darted off, twisting and turning with the speed of lightning.

'Ooh, beastly!' Cathie exclaimed softly.

John looked round at her with a furious face; his eyes flashed fire. Heaven help you, if you make another sound!

They pushed on.

As soon as they were behind the hill, he handed the baby to Louise; Lizzy was put down on the ground.

'You wait here for me. I'll be back as soon as possible.'

And he ran for all he was worth back to the camp where – as he had feared – he arrived too late for the changing of the guard.

'Where've you been hanging out? You weren't at your post,' growled Red Pete's deep voice.

'I fell asleep behind those bushes,' said John, trying to suppress his panting.

'That's *fine*! Splendid chap you are! Well, we can rely on *you*, and no mistake! Go on, get out! Go and finish your snooze in your wagon, milksop!'

John got out . . . to the corral.

Those scornful words 'we can rely on you' had hit him hard. Pete was right; they couldn't rely on him. He was doing his best to make fools of them all, and perhaps give them trouble and worry. But something in him rose up in revolt against that feeling of guilt. *They* had started it! They had become unfaithful to the original purpose of the journey, as decided on by John's father and all the others. *He* had a right to feel let down by them. *And* they had forced him to resort to this night's deception.

Sadly he walked across the corral, idly kicking the dry, trampled-down tufts of grass, and through the glowing ashes of a still smouldering fire of buffalo droppings.

He climbed into the wagon for the last time.

That was a difficult moment.

It was dark inside, he could hardly see an inch; but he felt so poignantly the desolation there, as something that assailed him from every dark corner, that a lump came into his throat. He peered about him into those dark corners. There at the back, Father and Mother had lain ill, and there they had . . . he swallowed and swallowed, he could not get rid of that lump. It hurt.

'Goodbye, Mother,' he whispered. 'Goodbye, Father We're going to Oregon. All of us. Goodbye.'

With a jerk, he turned his back on the wagon and all that was in it, and in one jump stood on the ground, on the outside of the corral. Then, noiselessly, he began to run.

The first pink, pale light of dawn glimmered above the mountains in the east.

6

The Snake River cuts its winding course through the Rocky Mountains from east to west, across what is now the state of Idaho. The landscape there is wild, majestic, massive. There, a human being feels very insignificant Gaping chasms, bottomless canyons, steep mountain slopes, gigantic peaks, and, in the lower regions, treacherous morasses and quicksands. Below the timber line, a wild vegetation through which it is often impossible to force a path; above the timber line, a grey, bare, fantastically formed mass of rock where only mountain goats dare risk their lives.

Nowadays, motor roads cross that country, and tourists drive up in front of comfortable hotels. From there they make trips up the mountains under the leadership of experienced guides, and every so often the hotel manager organises a 'camp fire', with music and dancing. The object of these entertainments is to give the guests a little taste of what took place there a hundred years ago.

But how the solitary scouts of those days, and the trappers, would roar with laughter if they could see it!

Or would they perhaps curse and say all kinds of nasty things?

Again, perhaps they might be proud, and say:

'All this has become possible through our work, *we* discovered these regions, crossed them, mapped them, some of us died here; thanks to us, emigrants came, brave men and women, many of whom likewise succumbed in the fight against insuperable difficulties on the way. But most of them remained alive, they got across the Rocky Mountains, and on the other side they cleared land and built farmhouses; they made the country habitable.'

The manager of the hotel, who offers his guests mosquito curtains, all modern conveniences, and cold drinks, is perhaps the great-grandson of a man who blazed a trail for himself through that mountain wilderness – a man who by day was at his wit's end to protect himself from the heat, and tormented by swarms of flies and mosquitoes; who by night lay shivering in his sleeping-bag, for there are already night frosts in August in those parts; who bivouacked beside a camp fire that was meant to keep the wild animals off him; who had very likely stood face to face with a growling grizzly bear, and yet had lived to tell the tale; who always had to be on the lookout for an attack by Indians, charging yelling down a mountain slope; who had to feed himself on the game he shot, or starve, and who was accustomed to suffering thirst for days, until his throat was as dry as cracking leather.

Through that country, the children wandered.

And they really did wander, for all John knew about the route was that they would have to cover three hundred miles in a westerly direction along the valley of the Snake before they reached the fur traders' post of Fort Boisé.

As far as possible, he tried to get down close to the river and follow it there, because there there was grass for the cow and the ox. But where the river flowed away green and foaming through a canyon, whose walls of rock towered up sheer from the water, they had to leave it and climb up, and find their way across the mountains.

Sometimes they came upon something that resembled a path; they did not know whether it had been made by wild animals or by Indians, and often the going there was so difficult that it was only with the greatest effort and with extreme slowness that they made any progress at all.

And then thirst also came to torment them.

In the baking heat between those grey rocky cliffs, sweat poured down their faces; they licked their salt lips, and grew even thirstier.

'John, I've got such a tummy-ache, and my throat hurts too,' Cathie complained.

Plucky little Matilda trudged on in silence.

Fat tears sometimes trickled down her cheeks; she licked them away, but tears are salt. She grew ashen pale under her sunburn, and John noted with concern the black rings round her big, dark-blue eyes. She is getting to look more and more like Mother, he thought.

Little Lizzy started every morning with laughing and skipping.

She slept like a top every night. She was a source of comfort and amusement to everyone; she did not see danger anywhere; as far as possible she was helped through difficult patches, and the first and the last drop of water were for her, though she was also allowed to share the cow's thin milk with Indepentia. Anna submitted faithfully to being milked, but did not yield enough to allow everyone a drink, not even half a mugful.

However, later in the day, when the burning rays of the sun did not cease to beat down on her red headscarf, and when weariness began to tell on her, Lizzy grew listless, started to cry, to roar, until John, tired and thirsty himself but with lips clamped tightly together, took her on his back and carried her for a while.

Louise walked without saying anything the whole day long. She never complained, but she never laughed either.

She was quite different from Cathie, who could sometimes be terribly tiresome, but a moment later could laugh and lark about as if they were still at home on the farm, playing, just as in the old days.

In the freshness of early morning, when a film of dew lay over shrub and tree, she would lick all the leaves, and then throw herself headlong into the bushes.

Louise would look anxious and say:

'Mind the rattlesnakes!'

Cathie would run on in advance, and a moment later jump out from behind a projecting boulder.

Louise would then pull a face like a scared old woman, and cry:

'Oh, Cathie, you gave me such a fright!'

But that was precisely what Cathie had meant to do.

John was grateful to her for assing about; it pushed

real fear into the background.

Francis was John's greatest support.

He had not the strong body and muscles of his elder brother, but he was tough and tenacious and very courageous. Francis's courage was of the kind that lies deep in the heart of anyone who has it. When it came to the point, he was perhaps even more courageous than John, though he would never have understood that himself. For all his spirit, John allowed circumstances to get him down, but Francis never did. He remained cheerful and lively; without him, the load of responsibility would have weighed very heavily on John.

As it was, the two brothers could still laugh together.

They laughed at the clumsy way in which Anna, the cow, and Walter, the ox, clambered and floundered about.

When the going was very rough and steep, John would take the little bundle that was Indepentia out of the leather bag dangling on Walter's right flank – on the other side hung a leather water-skin – for he was afraid that Indepentia might be hurt if the ox fell. In such a case, he preferred to carry her in his arms.

But Walter never fell; how he did it was a mystery, but he always managed to keep his unwieldy body upright, on those four legs of his, which looked so fragile. Now and again he did raise his head and utter a pathetic bellow, as if invoking the help of the cloudless blue heaven. However, help never came from heaven, but from earth; Matilda's strong little hands sometimes closed round his hairy, gnarled leg, and helped him find a good place on which to set his poor worn hoof, a place from which he could not slip back.

The cow was rather more agile, and quicker.

'Come on, Anna, come on, Anna!' Matilda would sometimes stand and call; and then Anna would come jogging across the rocky ground, almost skipping, with her heavy body under which the limp udder dangled. She tore leaves off bushes with her rough tongue, and sometimes chewed bark, like a mountain goat.

Nevertheless, grass was of vital importance to them all. Without grass the animals could not have stuck it out; and without the animals, the children could not possibly have carried all the baggage. Without the cow, Indepentia would have been utterly lost.

Whenever it was possible, John tried to go down to the river, which flowed through a tortuous narrow valley for a great part of its course.

There it was green, grass grew, sturdy cottonwood trees with heavy crowns even stood there; but the underwood was so dense, stunted willows and climbing plants formed such a compactly interwoven thicket, that John could cut a road for his little caravan only with the greatest difficulty. However, often it was in that very brushwood that they found tracks which they could follow – paths which had been made to and from the river by animals. When they found such a path, Oscar would always run on ahead, sniffing, and Matilda had to call continuously, in her high, piping voice, to keep him from bolting off.

Sometimes even John could smell the rank scent of some animal or other. He was always speculating as to what animals came along those paths, and what his little party might encounter.

There were many kinds of small tracks and imprints there. They might have been left by rabbits, martens, and opossums; the larger ones were perhaps the footprints of a wild cat or of a lynx . . . and what about raccoons? Would those comical, vicious little animals be found thereabouts too?

John saw many slots of deer and antelopes. He hardly dared think about grizzly bears, but he knew they must be there. He did not talk to the others about them, but sometimes, when his fear seemed almost on the point of overmastering him, and he really felt the need of an outlet for his feelings, he began to whistle, very loudly and shrilly, and that certainly helped. Or did it? He could not have said. On second thoughts, his own shrill whistling sounded rather sinister to him, in that densely overgrown wilderness, which smelt so strange and where you could never know what animal might presently stand in front of you. And so he would stop whistling. . . . Why were the others so quiet, too? Oh, thank Heaven – at any rate Cathie was beginning to complain about her tummy again! That sounded so like home; it was almost as if they were back on the farm with Mother. Tummy-ache . . . he looked round with a frown, to make it clear to her that she had to stop whining; but in his heart he was grateful to her for her commonplace complaint.

Down there, in the green dusk of the dense undergrowth, the children did not have to contend with that baking heat which gave them so much trouble up above. But it was stuffier, closer, sometimes it smelt musty, and there were mosquitoes. In actual fact, John did not know which of the two places he liked least. . . . And then, that constant rustling – it was swarming with game there, the animals darted off as soon as they heard the party approaching.

Sometimes birds of prey flew up out of the thick foliage, with a terrible flapping of wings. Very occasionally they would see the head of a deer or antelope peering inquisitively through the leaves, and then there would be a sudden loud cracking of branches, and rustling, as the creature sprang away with timid leaps.

The children were startled by all those sounds, particularly at first; but they got used to them. However, John, who knew that the region was not teeming only with small and harmless wild animals, always held his rifle at the ready, because you could never know what 'it' might be.

Towards the end of a day's march, they were dragging themselves along, but John would not allow them to rest and camp much before sunset. He was so obsessed by the idea that it was vital for them to hurry, to reach their goal before the snowstorms began, that he was almost cruel to his sisters. But also to himself, for when, during the last hours of the day, he hoisted Lizzy on to his back again and again, and carried her as long as he could, he sometimes felt as if his spine would snap.

At that time Francis, small and slightly built, striding along with regular paces and with a back as straight as a ramrod, always started to make remarks such as:

'I see . . . I see . . . a magnificent cottonwood tree, and underneath grows thick, soft grass. And it's on the edge of a small creek. The water there babbles over little pebbles, and the bed is of yellow sand, and in that water we're dangling our feet. And I see leaping silver fishes, which you can catch with your hand, because they're not afraid, since they've never yet encountered human beings. And Louise will fry them for us in the hot ashes of a wood fire. She sprinkles a little salt over them, and . . . and . . .'

He got no farther, but everyone knew enough. The queer thing was that those soliloquies of Francis always gave them courage, for they all felt that some such thing *was* a possibility; maybe presently they *would* find such a heavenly spot in which to rest.

One day – they had lost count of the date by then – they found, quite early on, a spot which absolutely clamoured to be used as a camping ground.

It was a big round open space in the middle of high underbrush; the grass was thicker and softer and greener than it had ever been even in Francis's most beautiful dreams; a mighty silver spruce tree stood there, which towered far above the shrubs and bushes, and whose lower branches offered blessed dead black wood, to feed the finest of camp fires. The river flowed near; a path made by animals ran down under the trees to a watering place; the ground was damp and soggy there, and bright patches of sunlight spangled it.

The children looked imploringly at John.

They were nearly weeping with weariness, they

wanted so terribly badly to stay there, but it was still early, that they knew – the sun was not yet low enough. Would it be possible to soften John for just this once? Their feet were swollen and raw from walking, their boots pinched, everything hurt, they were more tired than they had ever been in their lives. . . .

'Oh, John . . . please!' Louise pleaded.

Matilda had sat down in the grass. She was crying, with her hands in her lap. Oscar, who had been running about sniffing restlessly, almost feverishly, went up to her, his tail curled motionless under him, and sat behind her slender, bowed little back as if to support her. She looked round at him and smiled through her tears. The dog sat behind her in an attitude of keen watchfulness, with dilated nostrils and his head raised.

Francis never took his eyes off his brother. He was ready to obey any order he was given, but he wanted *desperately* to be allowed to go and lie on his back, and take off those chafing, torturing boots. Louise had an ointment for the open blisters (only John and she knew that it was just ordinary rifle grease).

John said not a word, but he nodded.

The animals were already grazing; he began to take their heavy loads off their backs. He patted Anna on her neck, just as he had patted his horse in former days – heavens, it wasn't even so long ago, either. 'Good girl, good girl.'

He had to find something to do, otherwise he would collapse from weariness himself. But there was enough to do.

First he broke armfuls of dry wood from the silver

spruce for Louise; never before had they come by their firewood so easily. Francis stacked it up, while Louise was already getting down to slicing off thick rashers from the last remaining meat of the buck which John had shot two days before.

'It's time you shot something, John,' she said worriedly.

'Don't bother your head about that,' said John. 'If that was all . . .!'

He was right; game sometimes crossed right in front of the barrel of his rifle, when he went on alone for a short distance. But he had no intention of killing wild creatures unless they were needed for food. Today they had reached that point. That was one of the reasons why he had agreed to camp for the night earlier than usual.

For that matter, camping was a great deal simpler nowadays than when they had still been travelling with the wagon-train. Now, in actual fact, it only amounted to choosing a good place and making a fire. For the rest, they all rolled themselves up in their own blankets; the little girls lay together like a row of sausages on a buffalo's hide, and the flanks of the party were formed by John and Francis, who took it in turn to keep guard and prodded each other awake whenever they felt they could no longer keep their eyes open. Sometimes both of them dropped off to sleep, relying on Oscar.

John most preferred a spot beside the river. He would tether the ox and cow close to the bank, and the children themselves slept between the river and the little rampart which John built up every evening out of the packsaddles and baggage. That gave him a feeling of greater security. And he saw to it that all the rifles were kept loaded at all times. They never pitched the tent, they were always too tired for that.

On this occasion, when the flames of the fire were burning up, he left the children behind in the care of Francis and Oscar.

Francis carried two pistols in holsters at his belt. They were much too big and heavy for him, but he could handle them quite well, all the same. His aim was not steady, but at any rate he would be able to frighten the enemy, if that should ever be necessary. Three loaded rifles stood upright against each other behind the parapet of baggage. They were old-fashioned muzzle-loaders; the ramrods lay beside them.

In his left hand John took the fourth rifle, the best and newest they possessed, a breechloader, and went out on the trail, carrying the powder horn slung over his shoulder. He would have dearly loved to have eaten one of those hissing slices of venison which Louise was holding above the fire, but he wanted to shoot more meat first. Then that would be settled.

He did not need to go far.

Close in front of him on the narrow path there suddenly stood a splendid antelope, with round, gleaming eyes and quivering nostrils.

The animal held its delicate head erect, and stood stock-still. Its long, straight horns stuck into the air, sharp as spears. John always found it hard to shoot down such a lovely creature, but he had no choice.

His father had taught him to shoot right between the eyes. He levelled his rifle, aimed, and fired at the very moment when the antelope lightly flexed its hind legs to jump away. It fell stone-dead at once; long shudders rippled across its skin – a beautiful smooth brown pelt with a thick black stripe along the back. The animal lay with outstretched legs. It was a young buck.

John walked back to the camp.

'Francis! Cathie!' he called. They would have to help him lug the antelope home. Fortunately, the distance was not great.

'Ooh, beastly – no,' said Cathie.

There! John gave her a box on the ear. Screaming her head off, she seized the animal by one foreleg and began to tug.

'No!' said John impatiently. 'Here – from the back.'

Together they seized its hind legs and dragged it to the camp; its head trailed lifeless and limp behind. Francis shut his eyes. John did not look at it, but Cathie stared in fascination; she found the sight repulsive, and yet she could not take her eyes off it. They were not real children of the wild yet. But they would become so.

John took his hunting knife, and with one sweep cut through the jugular vein. The blood spurted out, and Cathie held a pan under it; Louise always cooked black puddings for them from fresh game. She still had a little bit of flour, but it was almost gone.

John skinned the animal, and cut off its legs. Now, he did not find it difficult any more; the antelope had become merely meat.

Louise wended her way to the river, carrying the leather water-skins. She vanished down the boggy animals' path with the dancing sun flecks; a translucent green twilight hung there, and it smelt strange, almost rancid.

She came to the river, which flowed on broad and darkly gleaming, falling steeply as it went, foaming round projecting points of rock and round small, overgrown islets.

She looked at the steep, dark, shaggily overgrown northern bank on the other side; then she looked at the water close by, at the small streams that ran into the river, clear and shallow above their yellow bed of ribbed sand. She looked to the right, to the east whence they had come; but the grey rocky bluffs and mountain peaks were hidden behind the tall willow trees near by. She looked to the left, to the west, first up at the mountains, at their bare tops, one of which, in the distance, was covered with snow; and then down. . . .

There, in an inlet in the undergrowth, on a little sandy beach, an enormous bear with three young lay basking in the sun.

Louise's heart stood still; she caught her breath. Her only thought was to get away, noiselessly, without the bear noticing. But she stood there as though paralysed, she could not move for sheer fright.

A branch snapped. Slowly the bear lifted its head, looked round. . . .

Louise dropped the waterskins and ran, as fast as her bare feet could carry her. Behind her, the bear came splashing across the river, through the shallow water.

John was still busy with the antelope, when he suddenly heard a penetrating scream. Another, and yet another – close at hand now. They came from the direction of the river – it could only be Louise. There she was – screaming. Her arms stretched out in front of her, she came tearing along in the strange green twilight between the willow shrubs. Behind her came a sound of cracking and snapping. . . .

It was a bear, a huge, reddish-brown grizzly bear, whose ungainly body thrashed along at breakneck speed through the green tunnel of the path, which was much too narrow for it. The brute was no more than ten feet away from Louise; a terrifying snarl came from its throat.

Wagh! Savagely it launched itself forward; Louise had reached the open space.

'John,' she cried, 'help me!'

The boy already had his gun to his shoulder, but he trembled, he did not dare to shoot yet.

The she-bear was momentarily dazed by the sharper light, perhaps also by the camp fire, and confused by the many possibilities she saw there, after first having thought of only Louise as prey.

She stopped for a second, reared up on her hind legs, and mowed the air with her formidable paws with their great, sharp claws – a hairy monster ready for the attack.

And now two young bears appeared behind her. Growling, with upper lips bared in a snarl, and white teeth, heavy and woolly, they lurched along behind their mother. Just as the bear had been put out by the sight of the many children, so was John taken aback by the danger of three bears.

He only had one shot in his gun.

He did his utmost to control himself, he bit his tongue between his teeth, he *had* to save the children.

But he was not alone.

He fired . . . and at the same moment Oscar, the wolf dog, shot forward, and flew straight at the great bear's shaggy throat, bit tightly into it, and would not be shaken off.

The bear tottered. She had been hit; where, John did not know.

Francis fired his two pistols, one after the other.

A bullet struck the bear's left ear; dark red blood started to drip down its terrifying head. The monster roared, tried to get rid of the dog; there was a storm of white fangs and curving paws with vicious yellow talons, lightning swings, blows and growls. The dog yelped, but held on; the movements of the bear became more sluggish.

The animal reared up. Oscar hung on to her throat; blood trickled to the ground from an open gash on his back.

Francis thrust a fresh rifle into John's hands and he fired a second shot, right between the little flashing eyes.

The bear growled, gurgled, and fell forward, right on top of Oscar, who, howling, tried to drag himself out from under the colossus.

'Francis,' John yelled, 'give me another gun!'

Francis was already there.

It was high time, for the young bears were coming growling nearer; they lacked their mother's lust for battle, they seemed almost childishly surprised and stupefied, but they smelt blood and they were deadly dangerous.

The animals moved slowly, and were close by – an easy target for a cool-headed hunter, but not for a trembling boy. John lifted to his shoulder the rifle which Francis had pushed into his hands, aimed, and . . . the first of the two bears fell.

Suddenly, Cathie began to scream, and Lizzy joined in. At last the unbearable tension had begun to take effect. But it was disastrous, for John's attention was distracted, and that of the remaining bear was attracted.

Snarling, the young animal shot forward and made for the girls.

Before anyone knew what was happening, Francis had torn his red shirt off over his head, and thrown it to the animal. Instinctively, he had made just the right manoeuvre. The young bear threw itself on the shirt, set its white teeth in it, and tore the thing to shreds, worrying it until its curiosity had been satisfied. Then it lifted its head again.

But meanwhile John had seized the third muzzle-loader, and aimed once more. He fired, and now the third animal tottered on its feet; it fell to the ground, with a plaintive howl like a big, sick child, only a couple of yards from Matilda, who had remained sitting where she was, bolt upright, white as a sheet, and staring fixedly. Big tears slowly welled up in her eyes, as she looked at the bear lying in its death agony.

The danger was past. Cathie's and Lizzy's screaming and crying began to subside. But now Louise fell over on her face in the grass; convulsive sobs were torn from her cramped throat, her shoulders shook.

John had dropped his arms to his sides; he stood looking dazedly at the three dead animals. He should have been thankful, glad and proud, but he could not be. His knees knocked, he was trembling all over. A trickle of blood dripped off his chin; it was coming from the right corner of his mouth. Without thinking, he wiped it away with the back of his hand and looked at his hand in surprise. Then he felt that his tongue was hurting; in the terrible tension, he had bitten too hard on it. He closed his eyes for a second, to shut out all the light; he wished he could have closed his ears as well. After the fight, he longed desperately for silence, for rest.

Francis was the only one to run forward to help Oscar, who was still lying, softly whimpering, with his hind quarters pinned under the dead she-bear. He repeatedly lifted his head, but it fell again at once. Matilda followed Francis with her eyes.

Suddenly she saw him jump backwards and run off, looking distractedly about him. He darted up to the dismembered antelope and seized one of the legs. With that in his hand he ran back. Matilda looked in the direction in which he was running, and saw a third small bear strolling at a leisurely pace down the green tunnel of the little path. Sniffing first on one side then on the other, he rolled peaceably along on his stumpy, soft legs.

Before the unsuspecting animal reached its dead mother, Francis threw it the bloodstained joint of fresh game. Growling, the little grizzly shot up to it, worried it; then set its teeth purposefully in the meat again, turned round and jogged back with its prey. It disappeared from sight.

John, whose attention had been drawn by Francis's running to and fro, looked on in silence.

'That was just as well. Not one of the guns is loaded now.'

'I knew that,' Francis said calmly.

He picked up his torn shirt and looked at it contemptuously. Stretching out his foot, he tickled Louise in the side with his toes.

'I say, old thing, must I put this rag on again?'

Louise sat up. She laughed shortly. Then she looked worried once more.

'I'll give you another,' she said in a motherly tone, scrambled wearily up on hands and knees, and walked over to the baggage.

'Oh yes,' she suddenly remembered, 'the waterskins!'

'Where are they?' asked John.

'Down by the river,' she answered, shamefacedly.

Without a word, John set to and loaded all the rifles again, the new breechloader last of all. Then he took it and walked circumspectly down the path. A few minutes later he came back with the precious waterskins.

That day, the children dragged themselves on until deep into the dusk. None of them wanted to camp in the place where the three dead bears lay. When they left, vultures were already circling above the spot, black against the pale blue sky of evening. John and Francis carried the badly injured dog between them, wrapped in a blanket. He was a killingly heavy, limp burden, and slowly blood seeped through the blanket.

They went more than a mile farther on. They had wrapped their swollen, cut feet in strips of red flannel from Francis's torn shirt. They all carried their boots dangling round their necks.

The undergrowth grew less dense. When they finally decided to camp, a very narrow open valley stretched westwards before them, the end of which they could not see. Little streams dashed and splashed down from the mountain walls, and they fell asleep at last with the sound of the water in their ears like a comforting lullaby.

7

They lost all count of the days. They walked and walked and walked.

For weeks and weeks.

The nights grew longer, darker, colder.

In secret, John prayed that they would be able to stay down beside the river. As long as they could do that, they had grass and water at any rate. Game became scarcer. The mountain walls on both sides of the Snake grew more menacing, greyer, steeper. John eyed those towering cliffs in dread that a moment should come when they would be able to get no farther.

They were not hungry; he was still always able to shoot something. In fact, they had not even touched their store of bacon and pemmican yet. They did sometimes suffer from thirst, when, although close to the river, they had to toil along its high bank, without being able to get down to it. But then they would sometimes find a little stagnant water in hollows in the rocks, above which gnats danced. They bailed it out into their waterskins, Louise boiled it in the kettle, and they drank the lukewarm, insipid stuff.

Oscar had made a good recovery after his fight with the bear. They had rested for three days after that adventure, had slept a lot and eaten a lot. It had done them good, but they had been on the road again so long since then. So terribly long. . . .

Walter grew visibly weaker, but he still carried his

load with patient good humour. Sometimes he would sink to his knees, but then he would scramble up again and struggle gamely on. Round his neck his skin hung in wide, slack folds, and his shanks almost stuck through it, as sharp as arrows. On his knobbly backbone he had open wounds where the badly fitting packsaddle chafed him. Louise smeared the spots with rifle grease every night, and John slipped dry moss under the straps when loading up.

Anna, the cow, kept her end up magnificently. She got leaner, but also more lithe and quicker, and she yielded milk regularly.

Indepentia grew on it, even though it did not make her fatter. Her little face and hands were red and swollen from the gnat bites; she would beat the air desperately and clumsily with her short arms, but she could not keep the insects away. At times she wailed piteously; but, again, sometimes she slept for hours on end, for the greater part of the day.

Every evening, Louise put Cathie to rinsing out the napkins, at any rate when they were near water. Otherwise, the scraps of cloth were hung over bushes or spread out on the ground, and dew and the first rays of the sun had to do the washing and bleaching. Indepentia's back and legs were red and sore, in spite of the rifle grease Louise smeared on them.

'I'm so afraid it'll be gone soon,' she said once.

'That's nothing to worry about,' said John.

That day he shot two mountain goats, and picked out the fattest parts.

'You've got to have the what-d'you-call-'ems,

the sebaceous glands,' said Louise.

She melted them down and the result was a thick, yellowish ointment which stank but answered the purpose admirably.

The children grew thinner.

Their hair straggled over their shoulders, their clothes hung in tatters; Louise no longer repaired anything. But she tried to sew moccasins, as she had seen Indian women do. She used deerskin for this, and sewed with sinews which she had previously chewed soft and split. But she made hardly any progress; the first pair had yet to be finished.

The children were still walking in their old boots. John had cut the toes off all of them; the children's feet were too swollen and painful for them to wear them normally. In fact, the only way of getting the boots on in the morning was to make them sopping wet, so that the leather became supple and soft. In the course of the day it got dry and hard, and at night, when the boots were pulled off, they sometimes took with them the whole skins of blisters which had burst in walking, dried, and stuck to the leather. That gave rise to many crying fits, and Francis never used so many long, strange words as when he was pulling off his boots. John was silent, as always.

The harder things became, the more severe he grew towards the children. They became scared of him, and he noticed it. It hurt him, but he did not change his attitude. He *had* to be strict, otherwise they would get snowed up there in the Snake valley before the winter came.

Night frosts were already occurring; at night they all huddled close together, each in his or her separate blanket, with the canvas of the tent over the lot. In the west, the mountain ridges were already covered with snow; the number of white peaks constantly increased.

They *had* to get on.

John lashed them forward with threats and rough words. And they obeyed, for without John they were lost. But they grew frightened, all the same, and shrank from him. Even Francis did not always understand him. They did not see that he always demanded much more from himself than from them, bearing in mind the difference in strength.

Of all of them, he looked the worst. His dishevelled, bleached hair hung round a livid, gaunt face, with eyes sunk deep in sockets surrounded by dark rings: his body was nothing but bone, muscle, and skin. But the children only saw that he looked sombre and black, stern and hard. Nevertheless, Matilda still sometimes felt for his hand, and she could look up at him with eyes which said: 'Come, John, please, John, be nice! Laugh – just once!'

But he could not laugh.

Often he took Independia in his arms for consolation. He would walk on in front of the others, hugging the baby to his chest, his eyes looking into hers.

In that way he made a discovery which few boys of his age make – he discovered how remarkable the eyes of a tiny child are, a child that still knows nothing about anything, and, with its innocent round eyes, seems to expect nothing but good, and consequently calls out the best in people. And thus the round, earnestly trusting, grey eyes of Indepentia called out the best in John. He bowed his head, and sometimes hot salt tears dripped down on Indepentia's little face. He felt so lonely, and the task he had taken on his shoulders was much too heavy. Perhaps more than any of the others he felt a deep homesickness, a craving for the support and love of his father and mother.

But once, while he was thus absorbed in Indepentia, in his loneliness, he stumbled over a big stone, and fell, with Indepentia under him. She set up a healthy howl. . . . As a result, he ceased to permit himself even that consolation. From then on, he only took her in his arms when she was safer there than in her swinging travelling-bag on one side of Walter's skinny back.

The narrow, shut-in valley became marshier; it began to look like a swamp. For the feet of the Sager children, it was a blessed relief. Their shoes remained pliable and soft all day, and their feet cool. But the heavy pack-animals found the going difficult.

One day, the valley began to broaden out. The sound of running water grew louder. It looked as if the mountains were moving apart.

At the end of a long day's march, the children stood before a narrow tributary which flowed into the Snake at a sharp angle.

The Snake turned in a north-western direction. The strips of bank beside the river were broad and green;

the water, which was shallow everywhere at the end of that dry summer, flowed swiftly into the wilder water of the Snake. It was a pleasant scene; there were even forests of whispering yellow rushes, with dark-yellow feathery plumes, which glinted and became lighter in colour when the wind ruffled them.

The faces of the children cleared; there, it was much less forbidding and threatening than in the dark, narrow valley of the Snake.

'The ground's too damp for camping here,' said John. 'We'll go a little way back from the river, as far as those cedar trees under the mountain slope. Tomorrow we'll have to cross this. We've got to keep following the Snake.'

They woke up feeling fresh and cheerful the following morning. John had been out very early and shot three rabbits; Louise roasted them, and sprinkled a tiny pinch of gunpowder on them – a wretched substitute for pepper and salt. But it was a delicious breakfast, all the same.

John went into the river first, in order to find the best place at which to ford it. In all probability, the water would not come higher than his knees, but he tied a rope round his waist and gave the end of it to Francis to hold. 'You never know.'

He walked across the boggy bank to the river, and cleared a path for himself through the dense reeds – carefully, for the edges of the leaves were as sharp as knives.

The bed of the river consisted of firm, greyish sand,

which was hard and tacky. But no sooner did he stand still than it closed like a vice round his toes and heels. Quickly, he pulled his feet out, turn and turn about, and shouted behind him:

'Quicksand!'

He went on moving his feet up and down, and in that way made some slow progress.

By now he was up to his knees in the water; it came no higher.

'It's just about the same depth everywhere,' he called back over his shoulder, 'but the bed's probably all quicksand.'

The children sat and watched him.

Constantly moving, never standing still for a moment, he reached the other side. There, the bank was rather higher and more roughly overgrown, but free from reeds. He tied the rope securely to a bush of red willow. Then he came back, and tied the loose end of the rope round a cottonwood tree on their side of the river. After doing that, he took his hunting knife and cut a way, with wide, sweeping strokes, through the reeds which bordered the bank in a dense fringe. It took him quite a time, and when he was finished his arms were bleeding from many fine, shallow cuts. He walked back a few steps and splashed the ice-cold water over them until they ceased to bleed.

He joined the others again. Louise looked at his arms. 'Too sharp for the little ones,' was all he said.

'Francis and I will carry the baggage across,' he added shortly. 'It'll be difficult enough to get the animals over unloaded. They're too heavy anyway.'

Francis made the crossing through the icy water three times and John six times, heavily laden and never standing still for a second.

'Now for the animals.'

John made a soft clucking noise with his tongue, in order to coax them up to him. They came, full of trust. He patted their necks, stroked their noses.

Then he said to Francis: 'Cut off a couple of stout sticks, will you?'

He continued to pat and stroke the cow and the ox. It was as if he wanted to ask their forgiveness in advance for what he would have to do to them.

When Francis came back with the sticks, his face set hard and tense again. 'They mustn't stop for one moment,' he said. 'We've got to chase 'em along as fast as they can go.'

'Let Matilda go to the other side first and call them,' Louise suggested.

That was a good idea. Right, then – the small children first. John took Indepentia in his arms, Francis took the hands of Matilda and Lizzy.

'No,' said John vehemently. 'I'll carry Lizzy as well. She'll have to wait, that's all. Don't forget, Matilda, you must never stand still. Just go on moving your feet up and down, up and down, don't stop, not even for a second. And you've got to walk along beside that rope. If you feel the ground sucking you down, grab the rope. D'you understand?'

The child nodded. John was never really frightened on her account; she always obeyed him to the letter.

She also knew, almost instinctively, what was dangerous and what not. Now she walked, kicking out like a good little girl with her feet through the cold water, which came almost up to her middle. She did not utter a murmur.

They reached the other side in safety. John hurriedly tore up big tufts of dry grass, and began to rub her down with them. She plucked the grass out of his hands:

'I'll do it myself,' she said, and rubbed until her legs turned scarlet. She enjoyed it, and laughed. Her flesh began to tingle.

John and Francis splashed back behind each other along the rope. The sun was already high in the sky; hours had passed. John was tired.

Once on the bank, he gave his orders.

'Louise and Francis, you two must take Anna and Walter by the halters; I'll follow behind with the sticks. Cathie and Lizzy, stay here till I come and fetch you.'

The animals began to hesitate as soon as they reached the reeds, but a smart whack against the backs of their legs worked wonders. Once in the water they did not flinch, only when they noticed how their hooves caught fast in the treacherously heavy, gripping sand, did they become uncertain again. John never stopped hitting their legs, with both sticks, left and right. Francis and Louise pulled on the halters as hard as they could, ceaselessly trampling in the water. From the other side, Matilda called in her high, childish voice:

'Anna! Walter! *Come* on, now! Anna! Walter!'

The cow mooed anxiously, but things went well. And they continued to go well. Once they had passed the halfway point, John hardly needed to strike them any more. The flanks of the animals heaved with exertion, and with blind terror of a danger they did not understand. Of their own volition they did their utmost to reach the other bank as soon as possible. All five were immeasurably relieved when they climbed up it.

John would very much have liked to fling himself down on the ground, as he had done after he had almost got drowned with Charley in crossing the North Platte. But that was impossible now – he had more responsibilities than he had had then. At once he set out on the return journey. His feet, which at first had ached like anything from the cold, had now become numbed blocks of ice. And he was so weary that it was as much as he could do to constantly lift them up and set them down. But he got there.

He took Lizzy on his back, and motioned to Cathie to walk behind him. This time he did not repeat his warning that she was under no circumstances to stand still for a moment. To him it had become so obvious that he did not think of specially impressing it again on Cathie.

They stepped into the water. Lizzy was heavy. John laboured on, without looking round. Suddenly – he was already well over half-way – he heard a voice calling him from behind:

'John! John! Shall I catch you a lovely silver fish?'

He looked round. There stood Cathie, bending down over the water with hands outstretched, laughing.

He swore. Keeping his feet moving, he too stayed where he was, and shouted angrily:

'Come here at once, you nasty little beast!'

Cathie looked deeply indignant. She had just made him such a nice offer. . . . She tried to come, but she couldn't. Great fear could suddenly be read on her astonished face. Oh, yes – now she remembered! It was quicksand, and she had seen the others constantly treading up and down in the water – she had heard John telling them about it, too. Oh . . . Mother! She pulled and pulled. She could not get free. Her feet were fast, as if in iron traps. The sand had already closed round her ankles.

'John!' came in a small. pitiful wail from her lips, 'John, I'm caught!'

The boy, who had been red with anger, went as white as chalk.

'You're not pulling my leg?' he called in a husky voice.

'No, John, really I'm not. It's true – honestly it is!' cried Cathie, who was usually such a tease.

A pathetic little grin flitted across her terrified face. She felt herself sinking deeper, very, very slowly. She had seized the line lying in the water; John had untied it from the cottonwood tree. *She* saw the rope as a comfort and support, but John knew it would be no use.

'Francis!' he called hoarsely. 'Take Lizzy over from me!'

Francis let himself down from the bank and ran into the water. The two boys rushed to meet each other. John set the three-year-old, crying child down in the river:

'Run, for all you're worth!'

Francis seized Lizzy's hand; they ran. At the water's edge, Louise was standing ready with something red that was supposed to be a shirt; at any rate it was dry.

In the meantime, John had reached the softly crying Cathie. He threw his arms round her waist and pulled, tugged, pulled – as hard as he could. But he could not bring all that much force to bear because he had to keep his own feet constantly in motion. The sweat of fear stood out on his forehead. He gasped. A kind of dull groan wheezed from his chest, while he exerted all his strength and pulled, pulled, *pulled*.

'Ow, John, you're squashing me flat,' Cathie panted. 'And it doesn't help at all.' Her voice was shrill with fear.

'Be quiet!' John snarled. His brain was working feverishly. It was obvious that this was not helping at all. His strength was not enough.

With lightning movements he began to haul in the slack rope. He fished the end out of the water, wound it three times round Cathie's thin little body, and tied an enormous knot in it.

'Now you'll have every right to have real tummy-ache presently,' he said, good-naturedly teasing her by way of consolation, and in order to make up for his growl just now. Then he left his little sister alone. Without looking round he splashed off.

Immediately Cathie began to squirm and twist in all directions. It was such a horrible feeling, round her feet, and it was so tight. The calves of her legs hurt as if someone was pinching them very, very hard. She twisted forward, to left, to right, back, tugging at her legs. Her knee-joints ached from it.

Suddenly she lost her balance and fell over backwards in the water. John heard the splash, turned round with a furious face, and came back and helped her up again.

'Confound you, child, stand still, d'you hear?'

He trampled off once more, as fast as he could. He felt exhausted; it was as if hundreds of needles were pricking the muscles of his thighs. Finally, he climbed up that bank again.

The others stood waiting anxiously; no one said a word. Everyone looked on in suspense at everything John was doing, so accustomed were they to the fact that John always came to the rescue, always knew how to meet every situation. If only the poor lad had felt so sure of that himself!

He picked up the rope, told Francis to untie it from the willow shrub round which it had been fastened, and walked with it to the only sizeable tree which was not too far away, on the highest part of the bank.

He climbed up into it with the rope, selected the most suitable place where two main branches forked, at the highest possible point, took his knife and began to peel off the rough willow bark – the rope had to be able to slide over the fork easily. When it was smooth enough, he cast the rope over it, and climbed back down again.

He called Walter. The ox looked at him, but did not come. Did he still remember the treatment he had had an hour ago?

Matilda and Francis walked up to the animal, and Francis seized the halter. Matilda tapped his dirty hind legs, softly, caressingly. The animal swished his tail, but began to run. John did not even go to meet him, he was so tired. . . .

'Louise, the girth from the packsaddle!' was all he said. Even his voice no longer had any strength.

When he had thus got everything, he tied the broad strap round the ox's body, but left some play. The free end of the rope, in its turn, was tied to the strap with three strong knots. And then:

'Pull!' John commanded.

He gave the ox a gentle slap on his angular shanks. Francis took the halter again. He led the animal away from the river.

The rope began to tighten over the fork of the tree, with Cathie at the other end. The ox pulled, the rope was taut, the ox pulled even more, urged on by everyone. He had been used to pulling all his life – it had become second nature to him. The rope quivered.

Cathie screamed.

Nobody paid any attention. Of course Cathie screamed. And no doubt it really hurt. The rope tightened round her body, round her hollow ribs; it was as if she was being cut through the middle, but it actually did seem as though her feet were beginning to come free, albeit with tormenting slowness. It hurt so much that she thought she might scream rather louder without even being childish; but for some reason or other, she suddenly became brave, and screamed as little as possible. If it came to that, her voice sounded so queer across the water.

The ox went on pulling. He did not slacken off for a second, but the children on the bank could not see that it helped. They could not know that Cathie could feel her feet being prised free, a little, a very little at a time. But the child was incapable of calling to the others to tell them. She felt as if she was being torn in two.

She no longer stood, she half lay in the water; she did not feel how cold it was, her hands were clenched convulsively round the taut rope, her little knuckles were white as snow.

The children on the bank looked on in desperation. It did no good at all, they thought. No matter how hard Walter pulled.

Louise wanted to go into the water, but John forbade her.

'Have we got to lose another one?' he said roughly, at his wit's end himself in his ghastly fear. It would be a dreadful death for Cathie. His stomach contracted, he vomited, and remained lying face downwards in the grass.

'Catherine!' Louise shouted from the edge of the water. She found that this melancholy occasion called for the use of her sister's full Christian name. 'Catherine, if you die, we'll always think of you!'

'I'm not *going* to die!' Cathie screamed back in smothered tones.

They were so used to contradicting each other that Louise almost shouted, 'Oh yes you are!' But she checked herself just in time.

Cathie was now lying on one knee in the water, with her other leg stretched out behind her. She looked a miserable sight, but in actual fact she could feel that the foot of her outstretched leg was almost free. And the other was very nearly as loose. Though now the sand had also got a hold round her knee. She was still pulling as hard as she possibly could on the rope; when she did that the loops round her body did not hurt so much. Louise stood wringing her hands at the river's brink. She saw Cathie's hair getting wet, and how she was almost touching the surface of the water with her left cheek.

The ox pulled steadily on.

Suddenly he plunged forward. The rope was no longer taut and vibrating, Cathie was being dragged through the shallow water. 'Whoa!' shouted John, and Francis pulled the animal back by his halter. Walter stood still.

Half-choked, Cathie scrambled to her feet, dripping wet. Sobbing, she splashed towards land, nervously moving her feet. Hands were stretched out to pull her up. Oscar ran to and fro along the bank, barking loudly and wagging his tail.

'It was awful – it was *so* awful!' Cathie got out, in a

trembling voice, between sobs. 'Thank you all very much. Thank you.'

There was a dry towel to hand, there was sun, and there were warm hands full of bunches of dry grass. But that was not enough. 'Make a fire!' John commanded.

Everyone went to look for wood except Louise, who remained with Cathie. Even little Lizzy went picking up twigs. In a very short time there was a big heap, and the fire was blazing up high. Cathie basked in the warmth; the colour came back to her face. She laughed; those comical dimples reappeared in her cheeks, and she shook her long curls like a wet poodle.

'So you see, I didn't die,' she suddenly said to Louise.

It sounded almost spiteful, but they all laughed. That was Cathie all over: spiteful and cheerful, bubbling with high spirits, touchy, full of ideas, full of rebellion, full of unexpected cooperativeness . . . that was Cathie, and that was how they liked her. They had never realised it so clearly as now.

Everyone looked gratefully and gladly at John when he said:

'We're not going any farther today, we'll stay where we are.'

But no game came within range of his gun, and they had to break into their store of food for the first time. John did not like that at all, for he feared that the day would come when they might need it more than they needed it now. But when he saw the happy faces gathered round the bacon spluttering in the pan, he

smiled wearily. It didn't matter – the important thing
was, they had got Cathie back again.

8

Endless days of journeying. Walking, walking, walking.

Would there never be an end to it? Would they never get anywhere? It all seemed so hopeless. Or was it *really* hopeless?

He hardly dared to look at the line of wretched, thin children's faces straggling behind him. No jokes were ever made now, no shout of laughter ever went up; even Cathie and Francis were silent.

They walked and they walked.

On feet in which knives seemed to be sticking. On swollen legs. With hollow cheeks and necks like sticks above clothes which had been torn to shreds.

One of the worst things about the gruelling march was that Indepentia got filthy. They could no longer keep her napkins properly clean. The flies never ceased to swarm round her travelling-bag. Her little face and hands were swollen and red from their bites, her eyes had become slits. Nowadays she cried for hours at a stretch, but they did not even hear her, they were so used to it.

They were still following the Snake – it must be the Snake, they thought, for they had not passed any other, greater river. Nevertheless, John began to doubt. Sometimes he thought he was going off his head. At night, when he looked, in the light of the camp fire, at his brother and his little sisters sitting there exhausted, hungry, often thirsty – then he felt almost distracted.

He had done all this to them. So now he had to take them on, to the bitter end. He had to – he had to. . . .

Yes, they were following the Snake, but the valley was growing more and more difficult to traverse. The banks of the river were high, rocky, steep; for more than a week now, it had been impossible for them to get down to the water, although they constantly heard it rushing by.

The few places where water had collected in the hollows of rocks were the children's only salvation. Usually it was Oscar who led them to them. With his nose to the ground, he followed the tracks of the animals who went there to drink. Whenever he found water, he would bark. And John and Francis could not run up quickly enough with the waterskins.

The little troop dragged itself on. They always had rags wrapped round their feet now; they tore into strips their last reserve in the way of clothes, in order to do that. Round those strips, they wound strips of fur from the animals John shot. But he did not shoot much these days. Even the wild creatures avoided that inhospitable region.

John had ordered Louise to go extremely carefully with the stock of food. But she had not been careful enough for his liking, for the children often went to sleep hungry. So he had taken the matter of rationing into his own hands. And since then they had found him even sterner and crueller than before.

He it was who received the first and only pair of moccasins which Louise made. He had them because, as a rule, he walked three or four times the distance which the others covered, either reconnoitring or hunting for food. But the moccasins were also worn quite through already; he had wound strips of buffalo hide round them.

John felt the dumb, dull rebellion of the older children growing.

The little ones accepted the life they were leading, no matter how terribly they cried sometimes. They knew no better, they remembered practically nothing of other days; even Matilda had forgotten everything, she had become a real child of the wilderness. Exhaustion, hunger, and thirst had erased all earlier impressions from their little minds.

But it was different with the older ones.

They were capable of feeling a poignant homesickness for former times, for life with Father and Mother, for life at home on the farm and later in the cosy security of the ox wagon. They remembered only the good things, and not those things which had made life difficult at times even then. As far as Fort Hall, it had been roses, roses all the way, they thought; but after that. . . .

They never reproached John. If only they had! If only they had once let fly. John longed for them to do so. Oh, if only they would throw in his teeth all the things with which he reproached himself: his stubbornness, his stupidity, his ignorance and shortsightedness in embarking on this plan. Then he would have been able to defend himself − then he would have told them about Father's wish, about Father's burning desire that his children should grow

up in those blessed valleys on the other side of the
Rocky Mountains. And about Indepentia, who had to
be christened by Dr Whitman.

There was nothing for it – they *had* to stick it out.
Just imagine . . . suppose Indepentia should have to
die unbaptised, as a little heathen!

So they went trudging on. In silence.

With fear in his heart, John saw that the valley
seemed to be coming to an end – that high mountains
seemed to bar the way to further progress. It was
possible that the river entered a canyon there through
which there would be no road which they could take.
And what then? Go back? But that too was quite
impossible, wasn't it? Did the others share his fear? He
did not know. They said nothing.

There came a day when it looked as if they would
have to leave the river. Broad clefts cut through the
high bank. Ferns and inkberry bushes grew there. They
had to make a detour.

Deep cavities in the rocks blocked the view. John
told the others to wait, and went on ahead.

The nature of the ground forced him towards the
south-west. He looked at the sun; his eyes smarted
from that blinding light above the dark ruggedness of
the mountains. The murmur of the waters of the Snake
sounded softer and softer. He was getting steadily
farther away from the river which they had to follow at
all costs. But he had no choice. He went downwards,
ever downwards.

Then he heard a new sound of running water,
coming from the other side.

Suddenly, as he turned the corner of a cliff, he saw a white, foaming cataract a hundred yards in front of him. It was a narrow stream, gushing down in a bed much broader than itself, between two mountains.

Beside the stream, through the long grass, ran a distinct and fairly wide trail.

It was not impossible that wagons had come through there, long ago. But it was as clear as daylight that it was a trail made by animals, Indians, and trappers!

His heart leapt up with gladness. These were signs of human life, of new prospects. The stream flowed to the Snake River. The trail continued to follow it. Left and right, mountain slopes rose.

John ran along the track as fast as he could. Soon he no longer heard the waterfall, but, instead, the water of the Snake. He whistled loudly, although he knew that the others could not hear him. The trail ran straight towards the river. There was a wide open space which had probably often served as a camping ground. Traces of old fires were still to be seen – patches burnt bare, from which sun, wind, rain, and snow had still not yet been able to disperse the old grey ash completely.

It was obvious that here, above the mouth of the stream, there was a ford, and that the trail continued on the other side. And it was hardly possible for it to lead anywhere else except to Fort Boisé. They could not be so very many days' journey off now.

John walked back. When he reached the place where he had discovered the waterfall, he sprang almost more quickly up the slopes than he had come down them. Over and over again, he stopped and whistled. And once he fired his pistol straight into the air, out of sheer joy.

A doe jumped, startled, out of the undergrowth. He whipped the pistol back into the holster and aimed his rifle. . . . The animal halted and looked round; John saw a small dappled fawn lolloping unsteadily along behind her, its nose cocked up at an angle. He had not the heart to shoot. He lowered the barrel of his rifle. There were sure to be more wild animals around there.

When he got back to the others, who sat waiting resignedly – Lizzy with her face smothered in inkberry juice – they hardly recognised him. He looked happier than they had seen him look for weeks.

'I've found a trail,' he said, simply, 'and there's game here, too. And we're going to cross the river.'

The latter prospect was not so very pleasing to the others, but John's cheerfulness gave them some courage, all the same.

That night they ate rabbit and venison – as much of it as they wanted. There was plenty of clean, fresh water, a glorious camp fire was burning, they were not cold and they all went to sleep with full stomachs.

Next morning Indepentia was given a thorough clean-up.

She screamed heartrendingly as Louise softened the crusts of dirt with hot water, and bathed her face with cold water. John, who otherwise never wasted a minute, stood looking on like a perturbed young father. Good Heavens, how filthy that child was! And how thin she had got since the last time he had looked at her properly! Her red-scrubbed skin clung to her little ribs like a film, but her stomach was round and swollen, in contrast to her stick-like legs, with folds of skin hanging much too amply round them. She had sore patches on her body which could not be got clean.

After breakfasting on venison, they crossed the river without any trouble.

The water of the Snake ran swiftly, and there were projecting spikes of rock round which it boiled and eddied wildly. But it was shallow, it was easy to wade through at that point, and much less treacherous than the apparently harmless quicksand stream of which they had such dreadful memories.

'It's just as well we could get over here,' said Francis, when they were warming themselves again at a fresh fire on the other bank. 'Look!'

Farther downstream, the Snake forced a way for itself between two mountains. There, the river gushed through a narrow fissure, foaming like a waterfall. On both sides, almost perpendicular cliffs towered straight out of the seething water, far up into the cloudless blue sky to where the mountain ridges were covered with snow.

It was a wild, overgrown path which they followed after that, but it was very definitely a path. The way had been chosen well through that ever-changing country; they climbed steeply, the trail wound about continually.

★ ★ ★

They went on climbing.

One difficulty which no one said anything about, but which began to worry them more and more, was that they went farther and farther away from the river. And nowhere did they find any standing pools. Their stock of water was but small.

The animals suffered most.

The dog, the ox, and the cow all walked along with their tongues hanging out of their jaws like strips of dry leather. Walter, the ox, was the worst off of the three. He had already fallen twice in clambering up the rocks. The cow tore like a creature possessed at anything green she saw. She still continued to yield milk – enough for Indepentia and Lizzy.

But after her big 'bath', Indepentia had fallen ill. She vomited up everything she was given; it was terrible to see that wretched little heap of misery, wrapped in its filthy napkins. She cried weakly but continually, and sometimes, when she slept, John was seized with dread that she might be dead.

Things went on like that for three days. By then, the last waterskin was only half full. Louise doled out the water in a spoon, under John's supervision. He was more severe than ever. They all had swollen and cracked lips, over which they constantly ran their tongues, but that only made matters worse. Their tongues also became swollen and painful, and their throats were parched.

'If we haven't found any water by tomorrow

night, we'll go back to the river next day,' said John, tonelessly.

The others had wanted to do that before, but John had refused to listen. How would they ever get any farther, if they did that? They would not be able to take up any more water from the river than they had done to begin with, to help them on their path across the mountains. But now he too was forced to consider going back, even though he knew that if they did their case would be as good as hopeless.

That night John prayed for water.

He prayed with a bursting heart, more passionately, more entreatingly and urgently than he had ever prayed before in his life.

Formerly he had prayed because his father and mother had taught him to. He had never found it all that important. He ate and he drank and he slept and he prayed – oh well, he prayed because it was the thing to do, it went with the other things. After Father and Mother died, he had forgotten all about it. He had seen Louise do it once or twice, but that had not lasted long either. They had become so engrossed in other matters.

But now – suddenly he had thought about it, he did not know how it had risen in him so suddenly, like a burning desire, like the prospect of a way out, a ray of hope in the terrible darkness. Now he got down on his knees, some distance away from the others and with his back to them, and he prayed:

'Great, good, dear, mighty God, give us water. Give us water, please, give us water. We're so thirsty. Dear, good God, please, *please!*'

Still kneeling, he collapsed forward, his hands on his knees and his head on the hard ground. All he had strength for was to go on whispering:

'Water, please, water. Water . . .'

They slept that night, all the same, they were so worn out.

When they awoke they felt as if their tongues were sticking to the roofs of their mouths. They swallowed and swallowed, their throats seemed like to crack.

The sunrise was a vivid scarlet, and there were strange wisps of cloud in the sky. The landscape through which they were now passing was more open, less shut-in than it had been. They had climbed high. To the east and north the dry Snake Plateau rolled away, in peaks and valleys; to the west the chains of mountains were higher, and here and there white with snow. They formed one great fantastic drawing in black and white. John measured with his eyes the distance to the nearest snow-capped peak, but he knew he had not the strength to get there. Snow . . . melted snow was water. His tongue scoured over his cracked lips once more.

Around their bivouac, the vegetation was parched and dry – some short, almost brownish-yellow grass, some thistles, and farther away a complete tangle of thick-leaved cactus plants, which had grown densely together.

The cow walked round them.

Now and again she pricked her nose on the spines.

That gave John an idea.

He walked up to the cactuses, cut the spines from

the fat, fleshy leaves with his knife, and took a leaf back with him for each of the children.

'Here's a sweet to suck for everyone,' he said huskily, in a clumsy attempt at a joke.

But it was not so silly as it sounded.

They all began to chew the leaves. They chewed hard and long, and they got some juice in their mouths, besides a stringy, rather bitter-tasting mass of pulp. It really did help!

John went back to the cactuses, and cut off as many of the spines as he could, to enable Anna to eat some of the leaves. He tried to get Walter there, but the ox lay gasping for breath, on his knees, and would not get up. So John cut some leaves off for him too, and took them to him; but Walter did not touch them, only looked at John with wretched eyes. 'Stupid animal,' said John, stroking the folds of his neck. Walter was nothing but skin and bone. Poor creature . . . Oscar did not feel like a meal of cactus, either. The children chewed and chewed.

John looked at the sky.

Those wisps of cloud were peculiar.

They were getting bigger and bigger.

And there in the east, whither he looked out over a barren chain of black mountain peaks, the heavens remained red. Strange . . . the sun was already too high in the sky for that, anyway.

Last night, it had begun to blow, and as John stood facing the south-east, against the wind, he felt that it was blowing harder, ever harder. And then, perhaps, would there be rain? Were they going to have a storm?

Was that the significance of the wisps of cloud?

Gradually they were growing more like clouds of smoke – thick, feathery monsters, which came nearer and nearer but still clung to the horizon.

He noticed that the animals were beginning to get restive. Even the listless Walter raised his head, into the wind, and sniffed the air with dilated nostrils. Over and over again.

John glanced at the children. But for them, nothing existed in the world apart from their thirst and their rebellion against the day's march ahead of them. John could not stop looking to the east; he did not understand what that could all be.

Meanwhile, he began to break camp and pack. Francis helped him a little. But Francis had not much strength. Poor Walter had to be beaten to make him stand up. John would sooner have beaten himself. Matilda looked at him reproachfully. All that was left of her little face was an enormous pair of eyes.

It was as if a mist was rising with the ever more strongly blowing wind. But that was no ordinary mist. The children began to cough. They thought it came from thirst. But John knew it did not. He began to believe that he knew what was going on, yonder.

A tremendous forest fire was spreading across the mountains, across the valleys, from mountain peak to mountain peak, blazing across the Snake Plateau.

The wind was blowing towards *them*.

The mist, which was really the precursor of dense smoke, became more and more stifling.

At last the children noticed that it was smoke; their

eyes began to smart. Nevertheless, they could still see nothing in the way of flames.

The fire was still too far away. But John knew what was bound to come. Now they would not be able to go back to the river, even if they wanted to. He whipped his little caravan forward. He could hardly get them to move. He cursed and swore as only the coarsest men among the emigrants had done. He dealt out blows right and left, shoving Matilda and Cathie on with a hard hand. This time he had given Anna a heavier load to carry than Walter, even though she was their milk provider. Walter could hardly keep his own bony body upright on his four weak legs. John took Lizzy on his back. And they went on. They walked and walked.

What else could they do but walk? They walked with dragging feet, without complaining. They did not even have the spirit left to complain. John often looked behind him. One of the children coughed more and more often. The stinging and smarting of their eyes also grew worse. The cloud of smoke became more dense.

'It smells like real smoke,' said Matilda, whose senses were the most sensitive of them all.

John nodded.

'But where's the fire, then?'

John made no answer. He thought:

'You'll be frightened soon enough when you see it.'

Very fine flakes of ash, and even extremely small sparks, were beginning to blow over their heads. But there was still no fire to be seen. It was burning behind

the horizon, but it must have been
tremendously broad front. If the wind d
if no rain should come . . . what then?
THEN?

'John – look –' squeaked Lizzy's husky ....,
from up on his back. Rabbits were running past them,
fleeing in the direction in which they were walking.
There'll be more animals coming before we've done,
thought John.

It was not long before they felt the ground behind
them shaking. They could not see far through the
smoke; suddenly three huge animals loomed up, tall
and broad, galloping along, with enormous antlered
heads. The male, with the largest antlers, led the way.
Then came the female, and finally a young one, not
much smaller than the female. Moose! They tore past,
making for the west.

More animals were passing – they could hear that
from the ground; but they saw next to nothing any
more.

The rain of sparks became heavier. Behind the
smoke, the ruddy glow became brighter. If they could
have seen farther, they would have been able to make
out the flames by now.

What are we to do, John thought desperately, what
in Heaven's name are we to do? All the animals are
running, but we can't go so fast. If we were only above
the tree line, where there's no longer grass covering the
naked rocks, the flames wouldn't be able to reach us.
But to get there, we have to go higher, and the path
doesn't rise.

They were still following the trail, which could be easily seen, even now.

'We're leaving the trail,' said John. 'We've got to go straight up the slope.'

No one objected. What would have been the use, anyway? What John said went, didn't it?

They climbed and climbed.

John no longer walked in front. He had told Francis to go straight upwards, no matter what came in the way. He himself walked behind, to chase and chivvy his little troop on. Forward – forward! He did not care now whether anyone moaned or wailed.

No, that was not true . . . he cared terribly. But he cared even more about something else. They had to escape from the fire.

He told them what was at stake. Then perhaps they would walk better, he thought. He put it bluntly and roughly:

'If anyone wants to get burnt, they can sit down and stay here.'

They climbed.

They had seen no more trees for a long time past; there were still bushes, but they were so stunted as to be almost dwarf bushes. The fire was coming nearer. The smoke was growing stifling. It was like a red curtain. Behind it, the flames roared; there flared the burning dwarf fir trees, shrubs, dry grass – there, everything was consumed by the red flames; there, everything became black ash. John estimated the distance they had still to traverse as a mile. How much time had they? An hour? Two? It all depended on the strength of the wind. In the last hour, that had not increased. It seemed rather to have slackened a bit. God grant . . .

They climbed.

They clambered, panting, coughing, sneezing.

Oscar ran round and round all of them, with his tongue hanging out of his mouth; Anna, who was carrying Indepentia, scrambled gamely along. John was so grateful to the animal that he felt a warm surge of love for her, almost as if she were a human being. Now and again, he patted and stroked her shanks. Walter, alas, had to be driven forward with the stick – mercilessly. It was the only way of saving him. But it was heartrending to hear him gasping. His breast wheezed, sometimes he bellowed as if he was in his death agony.

On, on.

Lizzy became an unbearably heavy burden.

On, on.

Bare, rocky patches began to appear on the ground, but they were no more than small islands amidst a low, shrub-like vegetation. Still, it *was* a beginning, after all.

Higher higher.

Now they could not see more than a few yards in front of them. The tears streamed from their smarting, red-rimmed eyes. The red glow behind the curtain of smoke was terrifying. For some time past they had heard a strange rumbling; now that it was closer, they could hear that it was the roaring of the flames.

'I thought we were dried up,' Francis coughed, panting. 'But I'm sweating like a sponge!'

Bare, rocky ground, with a few tufts of grass in the cracks – they could not see whether this place of refuge was really big enough. Just a bit farther, John urged them. Come *on*, now – please! Just a little bit! The ground remained bare and rocky. If we don't suffocate in the smoke, we'll get away with our lives here, thought John. Are we all present?

'You can lie down now,' he shouted.

Everyone was there.

No, Walter wasn't there.

John called, Francis called, Matilda called.

No Walter.

'I can't go and fetch him,' said John. 'I can't see a finger in front of my face.'

It was no longer possible for them to get away from the smoke. They all lay flat on their stomachs, with their hands over their eyes, ceaselessly coughing raucously and hoarsely.

The wind did not go on falling, but something else happened. A gentle, high rustling note suddenly sounded above the roar of the flames.

Drops of water fell.

Raindrops.

Big raindrops. And it did not stop at a few. A downpour came that was as if the heavens had opened.

'Is this the answer to the prayer I said yesterday?' John thought.

He forgot that in that wilderness every fire, sooner or later, can only be tamed by that other force of nature, rain.

It poured, it fell in torrents, they were soaked through.

The smoke cleared. Farther down, a nasty cloud of fumes hung about; but the rain soon put an end to that as well.

It would be impossible to imagine a sight more desolate than that which then met their eyes. To the south and east everything was black, black, black, as far as they could see. Many square miles must have been burnt out. Here and there the short stump of a dwarf tree still stood. That made the scene even more dreary.

They were on a sort of terrace. And they could now also see that the spot at which they had stopped had not been safe. Somewhat higher, before the mountain-side reared itself up steeply again, was another such fold in the ground, and there grass and low bushes grew in abundance. If the fire had reached their resting place, it would immediately have spread across and on, up the mountain.

The children lay on their backs. Their thirsty, parched throats caught all the drops of rain. Their tongues stuck out like little red flags.

John went across to Anna.

He unbuckled the baggage, and ran with Indepentia's travelling-bag to a sheltered place under a big, overhanging boulder. Then he opened wide the two waterskins, the kettle, the pan. He took off his shirt and spread it out on the rocky ground; everything in the nature of a piece of cloth he spread out, and he called to the others to do the same. Francis, who at once understood why, did it immediately. Presently, when the rain stopped, they would again be without water, and what would happen then? If they could wring out their clothes, at any rate they would have something, even if it was only an inch or so at the bottom of the waterskins. But perhaps there were also hollows in the rocks in which puddles would remain.

Now they had to look for Walter. Walter also had waterskins on his back.

They espied him lying among some bushes, a big, formless heap, not more than fifty yards below them. John leapt down.

'Walter, Walter!' he shouted.

The animal did not even lift his head. God be thanked, the fire had not reached him either. It had stopped a couple of hundred yards away.

John came to him. He looked at him. He patted him, stroked him, walked round him, and saw his eyes.

The ox was dead.

Slowly, John walked back to the others, carrying the waterskins.

'Walter's dead,' he said.

Nobody answered. Apart from Louise and Matilda, who looked at him with wide-open eyes, the children went on drinking, catching the rain in their mouths, in their open hands; they sucked their wet shirts dry. A feeling of dull misery came over John:

'Walter's dead!' he shouted.

That startled them. They stared. They stared down the slope at the pathetic heap of bones and skin which had done them such invaluable service on their way. Cathie was the first to begin to cry.

Matilda said:

'Walter didn't get burnt?'

'No,' said John. 'He fell, and then his heart stopped.'

'Yes, Walter's heart's stopped,' said Matilda.

With John, she was the only one who was not crying. For even Francis was standing rubbing his eyes.

Of a sudden, Cathie began to laugh. Brightly, she exclaimed:

'Do you see how black we are? And Francis is getting stripes all over his face!'

Then they all had to laugh, whether they wanted to or not. They looked so strange, with black faces and red, bloodshot eyes; and where the tears trickled down, they left faint, wavy streaks.

'John,' Louise asked timidly, 'John, don't you think we might risk cutting off a few slices of bacon?'

'Bacon?' said John.

All the same, it was no wonder Louise thought about eating. They were hungry – and how! Now that their thirst had been quenched a little, they noticed it for the first time.

'Bacon? Walter's there too, isn't he? But no – I'd sooner . . . If you'll just be patient, I'll go and shoot something. So many animals have been hunted out of cover by the fire.'

He set to and dragged all the baggage into the shelter of the overhanging rock, out of the rain, which was still falling in buckets.

'Hey, give me a hand, all of you!'

Thank heaven, the powder had kept dry in its box. He charged the breechloader.

'You lot make a fire there, there's enough dry wood down below.'

He pointed to a broad, deep fissure, running at an angle into the side of the mountain and shielded by a massive boulder. They had a magnificent cave there. It couldn't have been better.

Having given his orders, he set out.

'Come on, Oscar!'

He climbed higher, for he not only wanted to shoot some fresh meat, he also wanted to spy out the land. The edge of the rock terrace they were on blocked part of the view. They had to find that trail again.

The dog began to bark, violently, almost anxiously.

From its bed on the ground, a cat-like animal suddenly sprang up with a lightning leap, glistening wet. A lynx!

John shot it.

It was a female. Then the male must be somewhere about, too, he thought, for lynxes are always in couples. He reloaded his rifle as quickly as he could, and looked keenly about him. He heard a rustling of wet twigs and leaves. Prowling along like a big cat, the male went up to the dead female – sniffing, with green, flashing eyes.

John fired for the second time.

The animal fell on its side; it was not quite dead. A moment later John fired again, between the eyes this time. Wicked claws, those animals had. Its flesh would be as tough as anything.

John climbed a little higher, to where a point of rock stuck out. He gazed to the west over the mountain landscape, in the grey rainy light.

His eyes remained fixed on one point, travelled farther, but returned to the same point. Always back to that one point, while his mouth slowly opened.

That . . . there . . . yonder, far below . . . that plume of smoke . . . and that – that square grey block beneath it . . . yes, it *was* a square, even though it was hardly visible against its surroundings in the rain-filled air.

That . . . that must be Fort Boisé.

Fort Boisé lay in the fork of the Snake and Boisé rivers. He could not see the rivers. But that meant nothing. They might be hidden in folds in the ground. That square, with that plume of smoke, *must* be Fort Boisé.

In a flash, he turned and ran down the slope, past the game he had shot. He waved his arms; his long, dishevelled, wet hair flapped behind his head.

'We're close to Fort Boisé,' he exulted, hoarsely. 'Two or three days off! Kids, kids – Louise, Francis, *say* something for Heaven's sake! We're close to Fort Boisé. They'll help us there. There . . . why don't you *say* something?'

He stood in front of them, dripping wet, with his naked torso gleaming and his ragged leather trousers sticking to his legs, and his arms outspread. They were sitting huddled beside each other in the shallow rocky cave, behind a small fire that smoked rather than burnt. They were hungry. They were not allowed to eat any bacon. They had lost the power to be glad.

Louise smiled at last through a mist of tears. 'That's splendid, John. But we're so tired. And when we get to Fort Boisé, we've still got to go on, haven't we?'

In spite of himself, John understood: they were too exhausted to rejoice about anything. But it was a great disappointment for him.

However, a couple of hours later the atmosphere was better.

'Lynx is the nicest stuff I've ever eaten,' said Cathie, pulling at the tough roasted meat with her white teeth, for all she was worth. 'The very nicest, nicest stuff!'

Night fell. And they went to sleep. John kept the low fire going; he had got used to waking up constantly, throwing wood on such a fire, and dropping off again at once. Some distance away, wolves howled. Oscar lay half waking, half sleeping.

Next morning they went on their way.

Walter remained behind alone.

9

One afternoon in September 1844 a boy staggered in through the gate of Fort Boisé.

In his arms lay a child.

The boy was dressed in nothing but a pair of buckskin trousers, which hung round him in tatters, and two bundles of rags on his feet which had once been moccasins. His hair, bleached almost white, hung in tangled skeins over his bare shoulders.

The factor of that one-man post on the Snake River was used to all the hard aspects of life in the wilderness. He had endured privations himself, and he had seen others endure them. But when he saw John Sager, words failed him: he could do nothing but curse, with horror and amazement.

John's first importunate question was whether there was a white woman in the fort. And that almost made the factor laugh. A white woman! The idea! No, there wasn't. Why?

John jerked his chin towards the little heap of rags in his outstretched arms:

'She won't drink anything any more. She brings it all up.'

The man examined the bundle more closely. He turned back the cloths. With a feeling of repulsion, he waved away the flies which swarmed down on it. Was that red, swollen, wretched little object a child's face? Its tiny neck looked like a stick; and when he saw its grimy, skinny little carcass, with the abnormally bulging round belly, he could not utter a word. What, in the name of God, could he do here?

'Perhaps there's a woman who'd be willing to suckle the child in the Shoshone Indians' camp?' he suggested.

But privately he thought that no Indian woman would consider taking in such a terribly neglected child. He looked at the haggard boy, but the lad's eyes gazed straight and firmly at him. A strange power shone from them.

'No, not an Indian woman, I can't rely on them,' said John, who was hardly able to stand on his feet. 'And besides, we've got to go on.'

'On?'

Yes, of course they had to go on, they couldn't stay there; the factor was the first to agree with him on that. But to go on was at least as impossible.

John turned, and looked up in silence at the ridge of the hill down which he had just climbed. The factor's eyes followed his. And one shock was succeeded by another. There came the rearguard! Sakes alive! How was it possible?

A dark boy of about eleven years old, lean as a skeleton, led the little caravan, which seemed to consist of a horde of little girls in such a state of filth and neglect as the factor had never yet seen even amongst the poorest Indians. Round their dirty, brown, skinny bodies hung colourless shreds of material which might once have been red; wherever he looked, he saw a bigger pair of eyes than the last one, in emaciated faces with swollen, cracked lips.

'No wonder,' thought the factor. 'Those children must have suffered hellish thirst.' They came from the bone-dry lava waste of the Snake Plateau.

He bawled something incomprehensible back over his shoulder, across the courtyard of the fort.

An Indian came up, dressed in a faded red pair of general's trousers which had strayed to the Far West and come down shockingly in the world. The factor pointed to the little procession of children, which was approaching the gate with dragging feet.

'See they get something to eat and drink,' he said brusquely.

But the Indian stood rooted to the spot, looking with open mouth. White children on foot through that desert! He shook his head uncomprehendingly.

John turned to Francis, who was now hobbling in:

'There's no white woman here.'

With difficulty Francis answered:

'Then we'll do it ourselves, with Anna.'

Anna?

The factor heard a dog barking. Shortly afterwards the head of a cow appeared above the brow of the hill, and then the whole cow came into sight; she was loaded and hung about with baggage like a mule. The dog ran round and round the cow, for she made no progress. Over and over again she discovered fresh grass. In their burning impatience to reach the fort the children had not waited for her, but Oscar, whose herder's instinct had developed more and more on the journey, had remained behind with her.

'What else have you people got, besides a dog and a cow?' the dumbfounded factor inquired. 'Is there perhaps a . . .? Have you got a father?' There was no mother, that was obvious.

John shook his head.

'Where do you come from, and how?'

'From Fort Hall, on foot.'

Yes, where on earth else could they have come from? But it was so grossly improbable! The factor scrutinised from head to foot that brown, bony boy with the child in his arms. A lump came into his throat, and tears into his eyes – good Lord, surely a man like him wasn't going to cry, was he now, at the sight of a fine lad? What was behind all this? The boy filled him with deep respect; his body might be wasted and dog-tired, but that firm chin, that resolute mouth, and that constellation of freckles on his nose . . . what eyes the lad had! He might have been a Roman emperor.

'Sir,' John asked politely, 'may we stay here for the night?'

Stay for the night? Sakes alive, suppose they *shouldn't* be allowed to stay there for the night! The factor nodded his head vigorously.

'Boy, you can stay here as long as you like, and rest, and eat, and sleep, and get your hair cut, and – but no, you don't need a razor yet. Heavens above, how's it possible? Come on, children, wash your ears, cut your nails, muck out your hair, fill your bellies, and sleep for three days!'

He pushed them in front of him, one by one – one

after the other they all got a shove, and in that way they landed in a spacious, rather dark room, where a square trestle table stood in front of an open, roughly cemented hearth. A couple of crudely knocked together chairs stood there, and the rest of the furniture consisted of packing cases and whisky barrels, which, when necessary, could serve as seats, ranged along the walls. In one of the corners lay a pile of skins. Rifles hung on the wall.

Oscar came running in wagging his tail, and Anna very nearly crossed the threshold.

'I take my hat off to that cow. Has she toddled along with you the whole three hundred miles?' asked the factor. He felt he had to say something, but he didn't know what; those children put him out, with their great, serious eyes, and famine-ridden faces. He wanted to have everything done on and for them, but he didn't know where to start.

'Where may we put our baggage, sir?' asked John, as if he was a tourist just arrived at an hotel.

'Chuck it down anywhere, chuck it all down here!' cried the factor, walking quickly to and fro. 'And you children go and sit down, too, for goodness' sake, don't stay standing on those shaking legs! Heavens above, what am I to do with you? What would you like? What would you like first, lad?'

'Water, sir.'

'You shall have it, you shall have it.'

He went outside and shouted something.

The Indian who had been the first to appear, and who proved to be the fort's cook, came up carrying two heavy earthenware pitchers. The water in them was cool.

The clear water dripped into the mugs through a little spout. The children fell on it. More – more, still more. Outstretched hands.

'Out of the question!' said the factor. He shook his bearded head. 'You've arrived safe and sound, we're not going to make you ill here! Steady on, steady on!'

He looked at John, who was standing to one side.

'Hey, lad, shall I hold that baby for you for a minute? Then you'll be able to drink too!'

Grinning, with a clumsy movement of his arms, he made as if to take the little bundle over.

'Will you be *very* careful with her, sir?' John asked earnestly.

The factor took the roll of rags. Good Lord, what a stench! He turned his head away. John saw it, and went brick-red with shame. He gulped down a cupful of water, and took the child back from the factor.

'She's very ill, sir. She fell ill after we'd given her a really good wash, for once. For some time before that, we hadn't had enough water to do it. My eldest sister would like to clean her up properly now if, perhaps, we could have a tub of warm water.'

He checked himself, swallowed, and said with difficulty:

'And then . . . then we'll just have to try her with cow's milk again.'

'Do you think weak, lukewarm beef tea would be any good?' asked the factor, smitten by a brainwave.

He looked shy; he felt unutterably ridiculous in the

role of nursemaid. He coughed and scratched behind his ear, in his thick, black thatch.

'And as for that tub – I'll see you get it!'

There was a separate washroom. An enormous barrel full of water stood in the middle. And quite a dozen big wooden tubs stood leaning against the rough log wall.

'When I get an invasion of trappers, they haven't the patience to wait for each other with washing, they all want to wash at the same time,' said the factor, who did not let the children out of his sight for a moment, as if he feared they might walk out through the gate again in that state.

'Splash around to your heart's content, here are scrubbing brushes and soap – it's not all that good, we made it ourselves out of bear's grease, but I don't suppose you're choosy. Yes, throw your rags down in a heap, we'll burn the lot. Perhaps I'll be able to get a pipe out of it. My tobacco's almost gone. Clothes, huh! Do you call these clothes? I'll dress you up in new things, the girls must just not be too particular, that's all. The Company'll probably not take it amiss of me, if I squander a few less pairs of trousers and blankets on the Indians in exchange for skins. And if they do take it amiss, I still don't care a damn –

'Lordy, Lordy, what a sight those feet of yours are! Hey!' he shouted through the open door of the washroom, into the sunny courtyard, where an inquisitive Indian was sitting on the ground before the threshold. 'Hey, you –' and there followed a flood of vehement, incomprehensible words.

The Indian got lazily to his feet and slouched off to the other side of the courtyard, where he disappeared in the dark store-room. He came back with an armful of moccasins. Only men's sizes.

'Better than nothing,' said the factor, 'and quite a number of those children's tootsies of yours will have to be treated with ointment and wrapped in bandages, anyway. You'll be surprised – I was a stretcher-bearer during the war. We'll freshen you lot up. You've got a nerve, you kids, to cross the mountains which the God of the British planked down here to keep the Americans away. I wish I could spare a mounted messenger to send to the English factor at Fort Hall, to tell him you've arrived.

'Lord above! Come on, there, scrub your arms! Hey, you, rub that other one's back! Little pups! You can't even wash yourselves properly, and you stroll around the Rocky Mountains!'

The children let the storm of words pass over them unheeded. It was nice to see a grown-up again, and hear him, even if he did make as much uproar as a child. His deep man's voice constantly boomed across the room; the splashing and floundering about in the bath formed the accompaniment.

Lizzy was taken in hand by Louise. She screamed like a pig being slaughtered, and lashed out with arms and legs. Of all the children, she looked in the best condition. She had suffered least.

Indepentia was wrapped in cloths drenched in oil. When the crusts of dirt had been softened, she was bathed in lukewarm water. It was a long business, but the result was a great deal better than they had achieved on the bank of the Snake. John, who stood by waiting, with red-scrubbed ears and short, dripping hair, in an old blue soldier's uniform with the trouser legs and sleeves turned up, got her back clean in his arms. He looked as proud as a father who sees his own child for the first time. Solemnly he stepped across the courtyard with her. He felt reborn; the blood pulsed strongly through his veins again, and he was as hungry as a wolf. Now they would get food.

The Indian cook brought in big dishes of meat. The children fell on them like little animals; they did not even take the trouble to sit down. Lizzy crawled up on to the table; but Louise found that just a bit too much. Holding a leg of meat in her right hand, she swiped out with her left and knocked Lizzy off. Lizzy, screaming indignantly, landed on the floor . . . with a sizeable chunk of meat. She remained sitting on the floor, gnawing away at her booty like a puppy dog.

John stood a little to one side, and looked on; with one hand he held a big lump of meat to his mouth, and with the other he held Indepentia.

The cook brought beef tea in a bottle. With infinite patience, John fed it to the baby in drops. Half of it she brought up again.

He was busy with her for over an hour. Then she fell asleep.

John looked at the factor: 'We must get on again as quickly as possible,' he said.

'Leave the baby and your two youngest sisters

behind in the fort for the time being,' the factor suggested.

But the boy shook his head. One thing was certain, for him; they had to reach Dr Marcus Whitman's missionary post as soon as possible.

'You're crazy,' said the factor. 'That child may die at any minute.'

The blood came rushing to John's neck and face; he went brick-red with sudden anger, and said something he should not have said. But in a flash he clapped his hands over his eyes, and began to sob bitterly. The factor turned on his heel and walked away. The lad's own tears gave him quite enough to contend with.

The languid Indian who had brought the moccasins came in with some wood and lit a fire in the fireplace. Outside, the sky above the courtyard was flushed red; the sun was setting.

When the children had eaten their fill they crept on to the pile of buffalo hides in the corner, furs were spread over them, and in less than five minutes they were all sleeping as if they would not wake again for years.

John and the factor sat in chairs in front of the fire. An Indian woman had come in and sat down against the wall. She was sewing moccasins.

'I've told her to make moccasins for all the little sore feet of those sisters of yours,' said the factor casually. 'She's my wife.'

'We really shan't be able to stay that long, sir,' said

John. And he thought to himself: a white man with an Indian squaw . . . ?

The factor must have read his thoughts, for he said: 'All the trappers have Indian wives. They're at least as good as white women.'

John thought of his mother's white shoulder, with Indepentia's little dark head against it in the dim light in the wagon. Strange – that it should be just that picture which would always remain in his memory. He said nothing.

'What do *you* know about Indian women?' said the factor, interpreting his silence incorrectly. 'A whipper-snapper like you!' He snorted in noisy contempt. Then he puffed out a tremendous, stinking cloud of smoke, from the mysterious kind of tobacco which he smoked, and said:

'Shall I tell you a thing or two about 'em?'

John nodded. He was dog-tired and sleepy, but it was only too clear that his host was pining to talk.

'I take it you know all about the rivalry between the British and Americans here in the north-west? And I suppose you know that there are two fur companies here, a British and an American one? Well . . . they frequently fall foul of each other. And how! One day, members of the two companies were camping not far apart, they happened to be hunting in the same region. The British trappers had a troop of friendly Indians with them, who set beaver traps for them and sold them the skins of the trapped beavers. The American trappers wanted those skins too. I can't say they behaved all that well, for they opened a whisky cask, just as they'd done before elsewhere, and as soon as the Indians got wind of the whisky the beaver skins went to the American camp instead of to the British. For, you understand, the rules of the British company prohibited the use of strong drink as a bait to lure the Indians. An excellent principle! But, as you see, the Americans weren't all that scrupulous, and now they got the best of it. The British, on their side, tried to intercept the Americans' food supplies. You can imagine, the two camps loved each other like brothers! Lord above, what a mess! For some reason – perhaps through some lark on the part of the Americans – the horses in the British camp stampeded one night. The animals went wild, reared, bolted, took to flight . . . and some ended up in the enemy lines, among them the horse belonging to the British boss's Indian wife; the animal had fled with their baby dangling in a bag from the saddle. Of course, the mother went hell-for-leather after child and horse, and it wasn't long before she appeared in the American camp, walked through it as cool as a cucumber, and took her mare by the bridle. At the same moment her eyes lighted on one of the pack-horses of her own people, which had also run over to the enemy, heavily laden with costly beaver skins. The Americans were already rubbing their hands over that stroke of luck; they regarded the horse's burden as what you might call spoils of war. But the Indian woman thought differently. She stepped up to her own horse, took the pack-horse by the rein without blinking an eyelid, and led it out of the camp with its valuable load. Well – I can tell you, there were fellows there who had their rifles trained on her, but the more humane and decent majority had their way, and while the men bellowed and shouted and nearly went for each other in quarrelling over what to do, the woman galloped off, complete with baby and pack-horse! You see . . . that's the sort of thing Indian women do. For she isn't the only one. For instance, I could tell you, about the Indian "Bird Woman", who rescued the whole Lewis and Clark expedition in 1805. . . .'

The factor swore. John had fallen asleep. And, look you, he had been spinning such an interesting yarn! The boy had nodded off and slipped half out of his chair.

The man took him up and carried him to where the rest of the family lay, under the furs in the corner. He carried him as he might have carried a small child, muttering one rough expletive after the other below his breath. He tucked him up like a mother, pushed the stiff, unyielding hide in under his back, murmuring:

'Tough little devil, splendid scallywag, whale of a lad. God grant that you and the rest of that small fry have a better future in store for you. Amen.'

In spite of all his cursing and swearing, the factor was a pious man; but he had got used to filling his loneliness with a lot of noise.

The children stayed at Fort Boisé for five days. Five days and nights of eating, drinking, and sleeping.

It was remarkable to see how quickly they recovered.

Their feet healed up; hard scars and calloused patches remained, but that was all to the good. Indepentia could keep milk down again; her cuts and wounds had closed, a new purple-red, tender skin had grown over them.

Anna had become firm friends with the three small cows in the shed at the fort. The first day, she had stepped over its threshold looking like some raffish adventuress, but she had since been scrubbed and currycombed, and once more resembled an ordinary, robust, common-or-garden cow.

John now saw the future in rosy colours.

Too rosy – they still had to cross the hazardous Blue Mountains, and at an unfavourable season of the year: it had grown too late. But the factor had promised to let him have an escort of three friendly Shoshone Indians, and horses.

And he had been given a map.

On the inside of a smooth, supple lynx's skin, the factor had charted the country: the course of the river, the mountain gorges and passes – he had roughly marked out the route with a piece of charcoal. 'Here, and there, and then again, here – and *here* you've got to look out. Seek shelter in time when snowstorms break; you can get hail-stones on your head of which you've never seen the like; and rain in which you'll get drowned. Camp early and carefully every night, and move as quickly as possible by day.'

John nodded. After all, with horses and an escort it

would be simply a pleasure trip.

The factor read the over-confidence in his eyes, and said:

'What the devil, my little man . . . don't stick your nose in the air like that. Bigger chaps than you, hard-bitten mountain hunters with good equipment, have gone into the Blue Mountains and never come out again.'

John mentally classified this among the many other tall stories told by the factor. He did not know that there was a great deal of truth in them. He was in a country into which only very extraordinary and courageous people had penetrated, and only extraordinary people experience extraordinary things. For that matter, how was he to know that his own history would become a tall story for the Americans who came after him? He did not realise that.

Nor did he realise what difficulties still lay ahead.

That night, the factor of Fort Boisé told him his yarns for the last time.

'Did you see Jim Bridger, when you stopped at Fort Bridger?' he asked.

John shook his head. 'He wasn't there. He was out beaver-trapping.'

'I can well believe that. An old hand like him can't lay off it. He's often been here. My word, the lies he tells! But you can take it from me, son . . . he only does it because people won't believe him when he speaks the truth. He's explored this country as no other man has, he loves the wilderness of prairie and mountain with all his heart and soul, and with all his liver and lights, as you might say. He's more or less flopped down on his knees before the great wonders of nature – but when he returned to inhabited parts, and wanted to tell people about them, they wouldn't believe him.

' "You're the biggest ruddy liar walking around on two legs, Jim Bridger!" – they told him to his face, honest they did!

' "All right, then," thought Jim, "if that's the way you feel, you'll *get* lies from me!"

'And since then he's been telling 'em – my word, how he's been telling 'em! They *are* lies, and yet there's more truth in them than townsfolk think.

'Jim Bridger discovered the Great Salt Lake. And he was more or less the first person to go right across Yellowstone.★ Boy, you'd open your eyes if you ever got *there*. You'd see rocks and mountains of the strangest imaginable shapes, weird caverns, hot springs, and fountains of soda water – I'm not kidding! Now I'll tell you something of what happened to Jim Bridger there. He told me himself.

'As I was saying, in Yellowstone there are petrified forests – petrified trees, with petrified birds. That's because a big medicine man of the Crow Indians once

---

★ Yellowstone Park is now one of the largest and most remarkable nature reserves in America. It is not surprising that the reports of the first discoverers of the region were regarded as fairy tales and lies. The strangest rock formations, wondrous caves, hot geysers, and soda-water springs are to be found there.

put a curse on a mountain there, and since then the grass, the sage bushes, the prairie chickens, the grouse, the moose, bears, antelopes, deer, and rabbits, have all remained there turned to stone, exactly as they stood or lay at the moment of the curse. The mountain streams and brooks, the waterfalls, with their mist of spume and spray above them − it's all been frozen to stone. Even the sun and moon there shine with stone rays!

'Now, one day, when Jim was wandering around in Yellowstone, he saw a bull moose. Carefully he loaded his rifle and pulled the trigger. The moose didn't even lift its head from the grass to show it'd heard the shot. Jim crept as close up to it as he dared, and fired again. The moose went on grazing. Jim fired a third, and a fourth time, with no better result. He was very near the animal now. He seized his gun by the barrel, lifted it like a club, and rushed towards the moose. Suddenly he banged into something, fell, and lay stunned for a few minutes. When he scrambled to his feet, he saw that he had run against a glass mountain, a mountain of pure crystal. And through it he could still see the moose grazing placidly. The mountain was a sort of lens, which made the distance, that must really have been many miles, look small, and magnified the animal on the other side of it.'

John laughed.

'I shouldn't laugh too loud, lad, if I were you − there *are* miraculous things there.'

Francis, who was sitting with them on a whisky keg, felt a delicious shiver run down his spine.

'Tell us some more!' he said.

'No, boys, you go and sleep. This'll be your last night under a roof for some time. But, talking about snowstorms . . . I'll tell you just one more tall story about Bridger. In the winter of 1830 – I went through that in the mountains myself – it snowed and snowed without stopping for months and months on end. For seventy days, Jim said. All the buffalo which had no shelter perished in the snow, but their bodies were preserved by the cold. When spring came, hunting was unnecessary. All Bridger had to do was pickle the frozen animals in the Great Salt Lake, and there was enough salt buffalo meat for himself and all the Indians in Utah for years. . . .'

The sun rose in a golden autumn mist above the Blue Mountains next morning, when the little caravan left Fort Boisé. John went in front with one of the three trusty Indians whom the factor had sent along with them. The boy was clad in buckskin from head to foot, and looked like an admittedly small, but nevertheless genuine, trapper. The other Indians held the reins of two packhorses, both fully laden. Louise and Catherine walked, but Lizzy and Matilda sat together on top of one of the packsaddles, tied like Indian children. Francis brought up the rear with Anna. Oscar ran to and fro, or trotted beside Matilda's horse.

The factor had done everything he could to give them the best chance possible. All the same, he trembled for them.

He accompanied them on horseback a short part of the way. When the sun stood some distance above the mountains, John shook his hand in farewell. He would have liked to express his gratitude for a thousand things, but all he could say was: 'Thank you very much!'

'God bless you, boy. Remember me to Marcus Whitman,' said the factor.

He shouted a few more orders to his Indians, turned his horse, and gave it the spur. A cloud of dust parted him from the children.

He muttered a few of his bracing oaths as he stormed in through the gate of Fort Boisé. Now he was alone again, with his squaw, his whisky, and his Bible.

That night he wrote a letter to his old mother at St Louis. As a rule he only wrote twice a year – that was to say, when the trappers called in at the fort on their way to the east after the summer and winter trapping campaigns. But he had been so shaken that he felt an urgent need to unbosom himself in his own language, to someone other than his Indian wife.

He wrote:

I've told you many remarkable things in my letters, but I've never had such a hard nut to crack as in these last days. A terrible story it is, but something unheard-of, something unforgettably impressive. That boy – that John! Our Heavenly Father himself must surely be deeply moved by the lad's vice-

fatherhood! . . . He was anything but an easy leader
for them, he excused nothing. When his nine-year-
old sister refused to hold the baby, he put the little
girl across his knee, and gave her such a thrashing
that she begged and implored him to *let* her hold
the child! He had to be severe, his task demanded it.
His nerves were constantly on the stretch, even
while he was here – he couldn't shake the worry
of the too-heavy responsibility from his young
shoulders. By Jove, he softened me up, too, for, after
they'd had a rest of some days, I sent him further on
his way under the protection of a few reliable
Indians and with fresh horses.*

When the factor had finished writing, his letter went
into the cupboard, for it would be another couple of
months before it could be sent off.

The children waded across the Snake River. The
water was icy cold. Soaking wet, they went on. A chill
wind blew from the north-west. Their route lay to the
north.

It was not long before John's over-confidence sank
into his boots. He saw how much effort it cost Cathie
and Louise to keep up with the party. But it was
impossible to make their Indian guides and escort stop.
They strode on ahead singing. Monotonous chants
with long-drawn-out, droning notes and a fixed
rhythm. They sang and they walked, they sang and they
walked. Even Francis was near to despair.

* This letter is still in existence.

'Make them understand they've got to go slower, John.'

'I've tried to make them understand that many times already,' John snapped.

'Try again, then!'

'Oh, John, *please*,' Louise implored. Her legs were like lead.

Cathie was holding Anna by the tail, letting herself be half pulled along. 'If you don't stop doing that . . .!' John threatened her. 'It's difficult enough for Anna anyway, and without her Indepentia's done for.'

Cathie reluctantly let go of the cow's tail. She walked with lagging steps.

'Come on, we mustn't fall behind,' John cried.

He shouted to the Indians. They did not hear. He tried to catch them up. He fired his rifle. That helped. With irritated faces they paused until, panting, he reached them.

With despairing gestures, he tried to make it clear to them that the children could not possibly move so fast. He threw out his hands and held them palms upwards, to signify powerlessness. He pointed and gesticulated towards the ground: please, please, sit down, take a rest, I'll fetch them while you're waiting. He pulled at his feet, and made a painful face; he panted and gasped and pointed to the stragglers: can't you *understand*, then, how tired they are, how heavy their legs feel, and how their hearts thump in their chests?

The Indians did not understand at all, or pretended not to understand. They wanted to get on, that was obvious. This journey with a pack of neglected, orphan white children was an affront to their self-esteem. The Father of the Fort had ordered them to take the children over the passes of the Blue Mountains, and then return. Very well . . . they would do that, after their own fashion, and they would return as quickly as possible. Even so, the business would take weeks, and if they didn't hurry up they would be overtaken in the mountains by snowstorms. No . . . they didn't care for this trip at all. And they didn't care for those white children, either.

They looked at John in silence, shrugged their shoulders, and walked on again in silence.

John seized the packhorse, which one of them was leading, by the halter. That suited them perfectly. Let the boy lead the horse if he liked.

The animal was heavily laden, and in front, across the saddlebow, the three muzzle-loaders were tied. John was carrying the breechloader; the three Indians were unarmed. Francis was walking behind, leading the second horse, on which Lizzy and Matilda were perched atop of the baggage, with Indepentia dangling at its flank in her travelling-bag.

The caravan went on. Jauntily singing, and with swift feet, the Indians raced far ahead. The children dragged themselves along, but John no longer harried them forward as he had been doing.

The trail was broad and easy to see. It led through wild, high hill country. The afternoon was waning; the sky in the west was already beginning to turn red. One of the Indians looked round. The children were not in sight.

They stopped. They were satisfied with the progress made that day. They would wait for the young whites and pitch camp.

They sat down in the tall, stiff grass.

Suddenly, the sound of trampling hooves was heard. John came trotting up on one of the packhorses, from which the baggage had been unloaded. He was holding the reins in his left hand, and a pistol in his right. His face wore its Roman emperor expression.

With the barrel of the pistol levelled at the Indians, he motioned to them to stand up. Stupefied, they complied. He pointed to the south, and intimated that they were to get going. He turned his horse until he was riding behind them. In that way he drove them back to the spot where he had left the children.

The Indians did not sing now. They walked with sour faces, and very slowly. John did not goad them on; he did not want to make them more ill-humoured than was necessary. If the journey had to take place in this way, it would become difficult enough as it was.

They camped.

That evening, and throughout the whole night, John and Francis took it in turn to keep guard; they had their weapons with them in their sleeping-bags. An uneasy company.

Next morning, the journey continued, with John on horseback and armed behind the Indians. If he had not needed them as guides – and that *was* necessary, for the trail had already forked twice – he would have preferred to go on without them. The escort system had turned out differently from what the factor had intended.

The other horse was now more heavily laden, and Anna had also been given part of the burden originally on John's horse.

There was no lack of food and water. The Indians set snares for animals, and foaming brooks and splashing streams dashed down from the steep hills.

The greater part of the slopes was densely, darkly forested; here and there tall cedars and silver spruce trees stood out in bright contrast to the other, needle-leaved trees. The weather was damp and dull. At night the little party crept shivering into their sleeping-bags. John found the night watch more difficult each time. His vigilance relaxed as the days went on. The Indians were not unlikable, but they were so strangely impassive and detached.

The trail crossed the Snake for the second time, after another track had branched off to the south-west, towards the Humboldt River, in the direction of California. If possible, the water was even icier than it had been on the last occasion. They had cramp in their feet. This time they lit a fire after making the crossing. The Indians had respect for John, on account not only of the arms he carried, but of his whole personality, which compelled respect, young as he was.

For three whole days they followed the eastern bank of the river again, but at a comparatively great distance away from it; their course lay somewhere more to the north.

John knew that they could not be far away now

from the vast marshes and the valley of the Grande
Ronde.

On the evening of the third day, they saw seven
blue-grey plumes of smoke rising behind a distant
chain of hills in the north-east.

Francis saw them first.

'An Indian village,' said John.

'Or a trappers' camp?'

'Not at this time of the year. And they wouldn't light
seven fires, either.'

Their three guides and 'protectors' had also noticed
the smoke. They did not seem surprised, but pointed
to it with vehement gesticulations. One of them began
to tear up tufts of dry grass. He put them on a stick
and, at a suitable moment, ran to the highest near-by
hilltop, and lit his torch there. The grass torch did not
burn long. But evidently long enough.

It might have been twenty minutes later that a
loud yelling was heard, and three Indians on ponies
appeared like spectres on that same hilltop. The Indian
guides down below gestured to them. They signalled
without words. The riders above galloped three times
round their hilltop in steadily widening circles, and
then vanished without trace.

That night, John did not feel easy as he sat beside
the camp fire.

He was not frightened, for it was obvious that the
horsemen they had seen, and consequently also the
inhabitants of the Indian village, were friends or
relations of the three guides, and, although the latter
were cool towards the children and not very friendly,

the atmosphere had become better rather than worse, owing to the respect they now had for John. No, he cherished no illusions; he knew that, even though he constantly mounted guard over all the firearms, those three Indians, with the help of their fellows, could easily slaughter the entire little troop of Sager children.

But he trusted that the influence of the Father of the Fort would continue to be effective – after all, the Indians would have to be able to look him in the face again; and, moreover, he knew that children's scalps were not valued by Indians. In some ways they had very strong feelings of honour. For these reasons, he felt fairly safe. He did not believe that any downright evil plans had been made; and he was right.

In that belief he finally fell asleep, tired out. He had seen the Indians were asleep, and he had the rifles with him in his sleeping-bag.

He dreamt.

Everything was just as it used to be. They were living on the farm again, and Father had taken him with him to the local town. John was riding his own pony, and Francis was perched in front of Father on the saddlebow. They passed through the village of wigwams of Indians who had come to trade. Little brown Indian children played in the smoke of their mothers' camp fires.

Father, Francis, and he rode through the gate in the wooden palisade girdling the town, and crossed the broad highway which ran round inside it in a circle about the little tangle of short streets and low wooden houses grouped together round the wooden church and the town hall. It was a hot, windless day, and the clouds of grey dust which were stirred up over the unpaved streets between the houses remained hanging in the air for a long time. When they sank, fresh clouds arose. They gave you a nasty taste in your mouth. But Father had promised the boys a glass of beer, nice sweet maize beer, in the Golden Wagon saloon. . . .

They were still riding through the dust. The town was busy. That was always the case at the beginning of the summer. It was a real feast for the eye there. Picturesquely dressed and painted Indians rode past on their ponies, enveloped in gaudily coloured blankets, with shaven heads and strange, dangling pigtails with knots in them. Sweating Mexican pedlars plodded along beside their dirty mules through the dense, dry, upward-eddying dust. Drovers on horseback sent their long whips swishing and cracking above the rolling, bobbing backs of their herds of cattle. Cavalrymen from the barracks walked past, noses in the air, with their sabres dragging the ground and spurs clinking. Farmers hunched forward on their wagons, their arms loose on their knees, let their reins hang, and peered suspiciously out from under their woollen caps – they seldom left their farms in the distant backwoods to come shopping in the town. French-Canadian *voyageurs*, paddlers of canoes up and down the great rivers and rapids in the wilderness of the West, sauntered in and out of the saloons, singing their French songs. They always came to this outpost of the civilised world in order to paint the town red. And the same applied to the noisy, drunkenly bragging

Missouri boatmen, and to the trappers, perched high on their horses, in their gaily fringed leather breeches and leggings – John looked at their brown, lined faces; at their eyes, screwed-up and squinting from the outdoor lives they led; at their hanging hair, which was as long as the fringe on their buckskin jerkins. Self-assured and dashing, with a supple seat in the saddle and knees like iron, they rode their horses down the crowded street. John admired them enormously. Even more self-assured, and vastly more respectable, two fur merchants strode along the houses beside the stream of traffic. They held silk handkerchiefs pressed to their distinguished noses; they wore high collars and long, tight-fitting trousers; on their jackets brass buttons shone, at which the naked Indian children, playing in the dust, gazed as if spellbound. The gentlemen stalked past them as though they did not exist, and their beady eyes looked around for another attraction. The fur magnates stalked on, under their shining top hats of beaver skin, and knew that the fate of many people in this little world depended on them.

'They're beginning to sing a bit smaller, all the same,' said John's father. 'They're not the lords of life and death they were, they're on their last legs. The millions which have been earned in the beaver-fur trade are dwindling pretty rapidly. Traps are still set for the beavers, but in Europe the gentlemen started taking to silk hats long ago. Beaver skin's not fashionable nowadays.'

A small caravan of ox wagons came up, slowly but steadfastly. The canvas covers, beneath which the eyes of white women looked out from under the peaks of straw sunbonnets, were grey with dust; inquisitive little children's faces came peering out beside dark, resolute men's faces in the shade of broad-brimmed hats. Silently and coolly, the men took in the noisy, colourful spectacle of this, the last town on the frontier between East and West.

John's father reined in his horse, laid a hand on the sleeve of his eldest son, and said over the top of Francis's head: 'Those are the lords of the future. They're the pioneers. They'll make our country, the United States of America, greater and greater – until it's *really* great. And you'll live to see it, lads!'

They watched the whole caravan go by, and Father shouted good wishes to the emigrants. John and Francis were almost choked by the dust that was constantly being whipped up. They were terribly thirsty. When the wagon train had passed, Francis turned his small dark head and looked up at his father. 'Come, Papa, please, can't we have something to drink now?' John felt his tongue cleaving to the roof of his mouth.

They rode to the Golden Wagon. And there really was a gilt covered wagon hanging above the open door, as a sign – in miniature, of course.

Inside, it was dark; there was a murmur of men's voices; the air was so thick with tobacco smoke you could have cut it with a knife, and there was a sickly smell of beer hanging about. Father, John and Francis sat down and ordered drinks. They were sitting behind the dark panes of a little window, looking out on to the

street. The same motley cavalcade was still going past
before their eyes.

Suddenly a very big wagon, drawn by six oxen, and
with a snow-white canvas cover, came by. The driver
looked decidedly grisly; he had huge, hollow eyes, and
no cheeks. In fact, he had a skull for a head. He was
wearing a woollen cap, and grinning.

Father stood up, and looked. Without glancing
round at his children he said: 'I've got to follow that.'
The wagon was travelling strangely quickly. Father
walked between the tables to the door.

'Father, your beer! And you've still got to pay, we've
got no money, we've got nothing!' John cried, in
dreadful panic. But Father walked out through the
door. Outside, he untied his horse from the post of the
wooden fence to which he had secured it, mounted,
and rode off, without looking round even once. Of a
sudden, the street was completely empty. All that was
to be seen was that white wagon, in the distance, with
Father riding behind it. He was already hardly visible,
because of the dust. The boys stood with their noses
flattened against the small, greenish panes of the saloon
window. And now they could no longer see Father, all
they saw was dust; in the distance the thudding of
hooves still sounded, and the glass was cold and hard to
their noses.

John was awakened by someone violently shaking
his shoulder. He heard Francis's voice:

'They're gone.'

'Yes,' John replied sleepily. 'And we can't drink the
beer, either, because we can't pay for it.'

'You're dreaming,' said Francis agitatedly. 'Wake up, John. They've gone off with the horses.'

'Who?'

'The Indians. With the packhorses. We've nothing left!'

John was awake in a flash. He could not say a word. He gasped and licked his lips, as though he could still taste the dust of a summer day in the civilised world.

Francis was now lying with his ear to the ground.

'You can still hear their hooves,' he said.

John rubbed his nose, which was sore. He had been lying with his face pressed against the barrel of a rifle. He could still not get a word out.

Francis looked at him in desperation:

'What on earth are we to do now?'

Suddenly John exploded; full realisation of what had happened had come to him. He sat bolt upright and began to swear:

'The scoundrels, the skunks, the dirty swine. . . .'

And a flood of ugly oaths streamed from his mouth – words not unfamiliar to the factor of Fort Boisé. John did not know himself that all those beautiful expressions had stored themselves so handily in his head. He came out with everything he knew, and it helped. It was odd, but it really did help a bit. Francis lay on his stomach and elbows in the dewy grass, supporting his face on his hands, and stared at his brother open-mouthed. When John at last paused for lack of breath, he said calmly:

'*That* wasn't exactly the sort of thing Father and Mother should have heard.'

'If they'd been here I wouldn't have needed to say it,' said John.

He felt ashamed. Now he was finished, he felt that it had not helped so very much after all.

'You'd do better to say what we ought to do,' Francis continued. He turned over and sat up.

'Throw some wood on the fire and make some coffee,' said John, getting to his feet. 'I'll go and look in the snares to see whether there's anything for breakfast. The girls will have to sleep on for a bit. If they don't, we'll have the usual grizzling to put up with.'

Francis looked at him reproachfully:

'You curse more than they grizzle.'

'You go and make some coffee, d'you hear?' said John.

'There isn't any coffee. And there's no kettle either. There's nothing. Everything's gone.'

John looked around. It was a fact – those shifty scoundrels had taken the horses with everything that was on them. The children had nothing left apart from their rolls of blankets, their weapons, and their drinking-mugs, which lay, together with Indepentia's feeding bottle, in the trodden-down grass beside the smouldering fire.

John's mouth opened. . . .

'Oh, don't start *again*,' said Francis.

He clamped his jaws together. But what on earth *was* he to do? He walked round the fire, kicked viciously in the ashes.

'Those moccasins have got to last a bit longer yet,' Francis observed.

'You've got a lot to say for yourself this morning,' said John. But he could not help laughing. Little Francis sat there so pertly erect and resolute.

And suddenly John felt grateful to him. He walked up to Francis, pulled him to his feet, put his hands on the slightly built lad's narrow shoulders, and said:

'God above, I don't know what I'd do without your help, you wretched little brat!'

Francis coloured with pride and pleasure. He laughed, but nevertheless he said primly, like a miniature schoolmaster:

'Come off it, John, you're still talking Boisé lingo.'

'Oh, leave me alone!' John cried, almost gaily.

And it was true, the boys felt really cheerful. The future did not look so terribly black to them. 'We've only got the Grande Ronde Valley and the Blue Mountains ahead of us, that's all,' said John.

The society of their Indian escort had irked them more than they had cared to confess to each other. Now, at any rate, that load had been lifted from their shoulders. Admittedly, the fact that they also had to do without the horses, the store of food, and all sorts of other things was bad, but they had been much worse off in their time. They were not hungry, they were not thirsty, they were wearing good clothes, they had weapons, and they were healthy.

'But they're dirty, disgusting rogues, all the same!' said John. . . . 'Where's Oscar?' he asked abruptly.

Francis went pale. They called and whistled. They walked aimlessly around. Oscar was not to be seen.

'They've taken him with them, of course!' John

hissed between his teeth. 'The filthy skunks! Indians are nearly as mad on dogs as they are on horses. Of course, the whole lot's gone to that wretched Indian village whose fires we saw smoking yesterday.'

'Oscar wouldn't let himself be taken along as easily as all that,' said Francis.

'So much the worse,' said John.

The girls had been awakened by their calls to the dog. Louise shook her dark hair down over her face, and began to rub the back of her head. That always woke her up properly, she said.

Cathie was the first to perceive that their bivouac seemed less populated than usual. She looked sharply about her, and then asked hopefully:

'Are they gone, those nasty men?'

'With the horses,' said John.

'Oh, Jiminy,' said Cathie.

Louise opened her eyes in alarm: '*What's* that you're saying?'

'The Indians did a bunk last night with the horses and with almost all the baggage. They've stolen everything. And Oscar's gone too.'

Louise realised the consequences of this better than Cathie did, and tears came to her eyes, just as John had expected. She said nothing.

Matilda and Lizzy, who slept together in one sleeping-bag, sat bolt upright side by side, with eyes like saucers.

'John's looking as black as thunder again,' Matilda pronounced, dejectedly. 'Has Oscar really gone?'

'Now what d'you think? That I'm joking?' John

snapped back. He minded terribly that the dog was gone, but, as always, he wanted to show it as little as possible.

At that moment, a loud rustling sounded, which came quickly nearer, through the underbrush on the slope against which they had camped.

Before they realised what was happening, Oscar came bounding into the midst of them.

He shot straight towards Matilda and buried his nose in her lap, boring and pushing away, with his back legs planted firmly apart under his joyously wagging hindquarters. His tail beat the air like a pendulum gone mad.

Matilda bent her little body over the big dog, threw her arm round his neck, and said:

'Oh, oh, there, there, are you so glad, Oscar, are you so glad to be back, m'boy?'

Lizzy clapped her little hands, and cried:

'Oh, look, *Sh*on, oh, just *look*!'

'My, how glad *I* am!' said Cathie.

John surveyed his little troop. He could not help laughing at them. Really, to look at us anyone would think we were a happy family, he thought, a trifle bitter and thankful at the same time.

A big, bleeding weal ran over Oscar's back, just in the places where the scars from his fight with the grizzly bear had left bare patches. When the animal finally let his nose be seen, John saw that its bridge was also injured. The Indians had tied his muzzle up.

'Poor old Oscar. *You* won't reach Oregon without a scratch, either,' he muttered, kneeling beside the dog.

He examined the wounds. They were not deep.

It really was a happy family which, half an hour later, sat down to a breakfast of roast meat, while Indepentia lay crowing on a blanket, playing with her hands in the day's first sunlight, and Anna's big, rough tongue tore at the wet morning grass.

'If *you* don't think it's so bad that they've gone, John, *I* don't think it's so bad, either,' said Louise, magnanimously.

'I thought they were horrid, nasty beasts,' Cathie exclaimed cattily.

'Don't show off like an idiot, child,' said Francis.

'You mind your own business,' Cathie snapped shrewishly.

'Well, you *are* crazy,' Francis answered, shrugging his shoulders.

'Don't start rowing, or I'll throw you out!' John warned them sternly. But he had to laugh, for the row was a happy row, no one really meant anything by it, and it was such a nice reminder of life as it had been in the past. How often Father and Mother had had to intervene, in quarrels!

'No rowing, now!' he repeated, with satisfaction, although it was no longer necessary at all, for the children had become entirely engrossed in gnawing the meat from tough, stringy rabbits' legs.

10

But it was anything but a happy family which, ten days or so later, after having followed the trail round the south side of the beautiful but swampy Grande Ronde Valley, experienced the first great cloudburst of the autumn at the foot of the Blue Mountains.

The rain poured down as pitilessly as it had that night in the wagon camp before Soda Springs. Then, even grown-ups had thought that the end of the world had come, and that they would drown in a biblical deluge. That had not happened; one lesson, at any rate, the children had learnt. But, on the other hand, this time they had to endure the terrifying tempest without any shelter whatever. Towering black and grey cloud masses discharged their load above the wild mountain region. It was dark; the streaming rain dimmed and veiled any and every beam of light.

Shaking and trembling, the children sheltered in a ravine, against a moss-covered mountain-side which was bare and greenish and slippery in less than no time. Not only did the rain pour down, but also the wild brooks and streams which arose everywhere. Whole shrubs and trees were uprooted and carried away; great clods of earth and stones were torn loose; everything went helter-skelter downwards, along watercourses which were suddenly full to the brim. The valley, encircled by a ring of menacing black mountains covered with fantastically shaped streaks made by the white-foaming brooks and hill streams, was soon submerged; clumps of brushwood stood out like black islets above a sea which, lashed by the rain, rolled and splashed in grey waves.

The rain cut and scourged the little group of children cowering in the fissure, sticking to the side of the mountain. They stood in echelon behind each other, like terrified sheep, with their faces turned to the rough rock wall, down which the rain gushed in a curtain of water. Breathing was difficult. The hard, icy jets of rain buffeted their backs; it was as if they had no clothes on their bodies. Stones and rocks were dislodged and sent rolling downwards, forming a source of real danger.

John stood bent over Lizzy, who shuddered between his legs, screaming with terror, and over Indepentia – a soaked little bundle lying on the ground in a sopping wet bed of dense dwarf shrubs. He stood with the palms of his hands pressed to the mountain wall, and protected the two little ones with his back, shoulders and head as well as he could. A small, sharp stone had hit the back of his head. The blood was washed away immediately by the pouring rain.

'This can't possibly last long,' he got out between clenched teeth, to Francis, who was leaning against the cliff with his face in his upraised, folded arms.

John and Matilda were the only ones who looked round occasionally.

Of all the children, Matilda had always been least afraid of the forces of nature. But now even her eyes were wide and black with horror in her dripping face.

Her short hair stuck to her head like a smooth, dark helmet, and she had even ceased to feel the water gushing down between her grimy shirt and her brown little body.

She stood jammed between John and Francis, and could see nothing of Louise and Cathie, who were crouching huddled together under the cliff, with their hands on their heads. Behind them, Anna lowed nervously without stopping. Oscar lay between her four legs; the water streamed down Anna's flanks and stomach, and splashed on to his shining dark body. He lay panting with open jaws, his tongue hanging out like a red rag, as if he was thirsty.

The rain pelted down. It hurt, even though the cold had partly numbed the children. 'Hail,' John muttered. Hail and rain together. The hail cut and slashed; their skin was beaten until it bled, but the rain washed all the blood away. 'Stick it out!' John hissed over Francis's head to the squatting girls.

' 'Course,' came Francis's smothered reply.

Pitiful, stifled crying sounded through the drenched fur of the little heap called Indepentia. John gritted his teeth so hard that they grated.

It *couldn't* last long. The whole sky could not possibly contain so much water and hail.

Distractedly John looked at the pile of sleeping-bags with which he had covered the rifles and the powder horn. What on earth was proof against this deluge? A feeling of despair seized him – they had been getting forward so nicely, they were no longer so terribly far from their objective, only this last mountain chain, and then. . . . But without serviceable firearms, and without material for setting snares. . . . Great Father in Heaven, what would become of them?

They were so paralysed and breathless that they did not even notice that the rain was beginning to slacken off. Nevertheless, it was probably because of that that John suddenly noticed something – another sound, another rushing noise, more irregular, creaking and cracking, ominous, a sound which swelled and grew.

The cleft in which they were standing had itself become the bed of a stream; they were up to their ankles in swiftly flowing water, but they only knew that because they could see it, on the rare occasions when they were not keeping their eyes tightly closed.

John now saw that the water was beginning to rise; grey earth came along with it, stones, torn-off branches, fragments of roots with long strands like hair behind them. And when he looked farther up, towards where the pouring water came from, he saw the top of a great tree come sliding slowly down; the branches scraped cracking and creaking against the side of the mountain.

Slowly, slowly, the tree slid forward. The water flowed foaming and boiling under it. But it was possible that it would suddenly come loose – fifty yards or so towards the top from where the children were standing the sides of the ravine parted more widely; propelled by the water, the timber colossus might develop such great speed there that the children would not be able to get clear in time. The way down was difficult. They could not descend very quickly;

besides, it was treacherously slippery everywhere.

The other side of the ravine was less steep than that against which they were sheltering. It was their only chance.

'Francis!' John shouted. He pointed to the inexorably approaching tree. 'We've got to get up on the other side. You go in front. I'll come last.'

Without a word, Francis took Lizzy's hand and jumped over the stones, through the running water, to the other side. John pushed Louise and Cathie forward, and gave Matilda a hard shove, sending her behind Lizzy:

'Go on, go on, climb, climb up, keep behind Francis, hold on tight to the bushes!'

He himself seized Indepentia in his left arm, pushed the others onward with his right, and hoisted himself up behind them. They clambered on all fours, but sometimes they slid back.

John measured the distance; he measured the height and breadth of the monster tree, which was steadily sliding forward, filling the ravine with a terrifying cracking of rending boughs, and a rustling of leaves. The children were high enough now, he thought. They were safe.

The mass of branches came nearer and nearer to the place where the ravine widened. The guns and sleeping-bags were still lying down below, and there stood Anna bellowing for help at the foot of the slope; she was standing with her forefeet on a boulder, and the water was spattering up round her legs. Oscar, who had run after the children, stood barking above John's head.

'Come on, take this!' John pushed Indepentia into Cathie's arms. 'Hold her tight, mind!'

He slid down at a speed which no mountain stream could have emulated. Up to his knees in the steadily rising water, he seized the sleeping-bags and threw them as far as he could up the slope, to where they were caught by the brushwood. He grabbed the rifles, slung two over his shoulders and let the third one lie. He picked up the powder horn and chucked it upwards; it landed close to Francis. He took Anna by the rein round her neck, and hauled her along – the poor beast was so docile, and so eager to get to the children. She climbed so valiantly, too. John pulled as hard as he could, digging in his heels, and holding on tight to bushes.

The tree reached the opening and stuck there, instead of suddenly shooting through it. A projecting point of rock barred its way. The water foamed and seethed more and more violently.

'It's stopped raining!' Cathie suddenly screamed.

John looked up. Open-mouthed. He had not noticed that the sky was clearing, so intense had been his absorption in the danger that had menaced them.

And yet Anna was still not safe. That tree could start moving again at any minute.

John pulled and pulled, as hard as he could. Now that it was no longer raining, renewed courage gave him double strength.

Francis had walked down some distance, to collect the sleeping-bags. The girls lay on their stomachs on a sort of little plateau, holding their arms out to take them from him. Only Matilda kept her eyes fixed on Anna, who was advancing slowly but surely.

'Anna, Anna, don't fall, come on, Anna, Anna,' she went on calling.

The cow was high enough now, but she climbed stubbornly on, in order to get close to the children.

John was just on the point of going down again to rescue that precious third rifle when suddenly there came a noise as if lightning had struck somewhere.

With rending violence the tree tore loose and slid down the ravine, sweeping in front of it everything that lay in its path. With an ear-splitting din of scraping, creaking, bursting, and breaking, it slid below the children, slid past them. Speechless, they watched it go.

Seen from behind, the dangerous monster looked like a pathetic, felled giant, lying powerless with its naked, maltreated roots in the air. Quicker and quicker, it shot downwards; they only breathed again when it had disappeared from sight.

'Your head's bleeding, John,' said Cathie.

John brushed the back of his head with his hand. It was a small, shallow flesh wound.

The weather had cleared. The sun was even breaking through the clouds. It was a bright, still warm, autumn sun, which made the mountain slopes steam and smoke.

But the children were shivering. If possible, they were colder than they had been when the rain was at its worst. Their heavy clothes stuck to them like chafing suits of armour. Their hair still dripped. There was nothing with which they could rub themselves dry. Trembling, the little girls cried. Cathie tried to be brave, but her chin twitched and shook.

'Keep moving!' John ordered them. 'Don't stop. Climb up and down a bit. I'm going to have a look around.'

When he came back, an hour later, he found an absolutely wretched little bunch of children, huddled on top of and under and beside each other. Only Francis was walking about, round and round his sisters, round and round, like a sheep dog round its sheep. But he was purple with cold.

John scattered the group:

'Come on now, look alive – we're going a bit farther up. Louise! Don't be such a sickening baby.'

The poor child stood there with chattering teeth. And she really was doing her best to control herself.

'Get a move on, there's a slope up there which is right in the sun, out of the wind, and complete with a clothes horse for our things.'

Cathie was the only one who managed to get out a pathetic laugh.

'Anyway, I'm glad to hear whinnying again,' said Francis.

Like a brood of bedraggled, hapless chicks, they limped along behind John.

The spot to which he brought them really was more favourably situated than they had dared to hope. It was sheltered and sunny; the tops of the low cranberry bushes were already dry. The slope was so steep that the comparatively low sun shone almost perpendicularly on to it. Even the mist was warm there, warmer than their benumbed bodies.

John pointed proudly to the 'clothes horse' – an old dead tree, lying diagonally across a gigantic boulder. Perhaps it had been lying there like that for decades; the long ribs of wood lay bare, and grey with age. Its branches stuck up in the air, silver-grey from wind and weather.

'That's what we'll hang our clothes on,' said John. By way of giving an example, he began to throw everything off. A few minutes later, the entire wash was hanging to dry.

Lizzy had quite forgotten all the misery, and was running around stark naked, squealing with delight. John was busy rubbing Indepentia, rubbing, rubbing, rubbing her, until her whole tiny body was a fiery red. He did not care at all now how much she screamed. She had to get warm.

On John's orders, Francis had cut masses of thin twigs from the bushes and shrubs, and had stripped the leaves off them; he gave each of the children one such bunch: 'Go on, beat each other! Beat each other!' he ordered them.

'The one who gets reddest gets a prize!' John called. Tough little devils, he thought proudly, looking at his brother and sisters as they ran about waving their bunches of twigs.

Louise was the only one who did not join in; she stood a short distance to one side, beating her legs – the part of her which needed it least.

'Go on, Louise, or I'll come and give you such a doing,' John warned her.

With a shout, Francis leapt toward her, 'birch' upraised. She fled like a doe. John laughed until he shook, kneeling on the ground with Indepentia in his arms. He rocked her to and fro, and she stopped crying. He walked over the clothes horse, and reached up – his own shirt was dry already. He wrapped the child in it. Then it was time to think of himself. He started rolling like a foal among the rough cranberry bushes; in less than a minute he was red as fire and covered with scratches. And warm.

The children's shirts were the first things to dry. They capered round in those dirty-white, shapeless garments. Cathie had won the prize. She glowed from top to toe, her ears burned, her toes tingled. She became quite still with ecstasy when John handed her a mug of milk from Anna. 'Oooooh,' was all she said.

The watertight tinderbox in John's belt really had remained watertight. And the wood of the dead tree was dry enough to use, too, by now.

When a good fire was blazing, they remembered that they were hungry. But there was nothing to eat.

'My powder has got to get bone-dry first,' said John.

They had spread the sleeping-bags out in the sun. John shook the contents of the powder horn out on to one of them. He tore a strip off his shirt, and began to take the firearms to pieces and dry them. He frowned.

'I think I'd better set a few snares, to begin with,' he said, and walked over to the strips of goatskin, which were hanging from his belt on the tree.

'But you've got no bait,' said Francis.

'No, I've got no bait,' said John.

He ripped another piece off his shirt, and dabbed the back of his head, which was still bleeding. But the blood had almost ceased to flow. He took his knife, turned round, shut his eyes, and gave himself a good cut in the thigh. He staunched the blood with the piece of cloth.

'Now I've got bait. This'll fetch 'em,' he said.

Francis looked at him admiringly.

'Won't you please take some of mine, too, John?' he asked.

'Your blood's too young,' said John scornfully. 'It's got no scent.'

'My blood's got a splendid scent,' Francis flared up.

'I tell you, I can't use it,' John said harshly.

He went off with his leather thongs and his strange bait.

More and more items of clothing got dry. John was away a long time; and when he returned, they were all fully dressed. He was carrying something in his arms. A big wood pigeon – probably old and tough. 'Killed by the hail,' he said. There was just enough to give everyone a morsel of roast meat. John set a last snare and put the skeleton down beside it.

With faces and hands covered with red weals from the hail and scratches from the twigs, they sat together in the twilight, in the ruddy glow of the fire. They ate some of the hard, acid cranberries. Lizzy and Indepentia had had some milk. Heaven grant they might keep that power of recovery which Fort Boisé had given them, for some time longer, John thought to himself.

The sleeping-bags were still damp, but they crept into them all the same, two by two, as close as possible to the fire. And they slept soundly through the howling of the wolves.

11

That cloudburst had only been a foretaste of what was to come. The children tramped through wild country of deep chasms and of treacherous clefts hidden under dense brushwood; of turbulent streams and of slopes which were so thickly overgrown as to be quite impossible to traverse here and there.

They pushed on farther and farther to the northwest, setting their course by the sun; they tramped across hills and through narrow defiles; they wandered around for hours, sometimes for days, before they could get any farther – so impassable was the terrain, very often, and so unfindable was any trail.

Showers of rain and hail and blinding snowstorms hammered them, demoralised them, broke them. It froze every night these days. Their moccasins were worn out; they had wound strips of wolf's skin round their feet, but that was not enough. In the higher regions they waded through deep snow up to their knees, up to their hips. John always walked three times as far as the others; he carried Lizzy and Indepentia by turns.

The children were hungry.

The pistols and rifles had become unserviceable. After that first terrible downpour, John had not been able to get them right again; they had been left behind as old iron. All except the breechloader; that still worked, though not always – sometimes it misfired. It was now an unreliable weapon. But they had to use it sparingly anyway, for there was not much powder left.

John had shot a couple of wolves, and once he had killed a lean mountain goat. They set traps and snares, but they seldom caught anything. Sometimes they found only a skeleton, next morning – in that case, some other hungry animal had come by its prey easily for once. They drank rainwater and melted snow. Their feet froze, swelled up, and open cuts and wounds came on them, which got dirty.

The cow grew thin; her ribs stuck out like sticks. Nevertheless, she still yielded a very little milk. She fed on tufts of grass – the children scraped the snow away for her where that was necessary; and she also ate moss.

They were only covering five or six miles a day nowadays.

John walked ahead with black-ringed, dispirited eyes. Why, oh why, was one mountain ridge always followed by another? The children straggled along behind him, dull with despair, listless with exhaustion. They dragged themselves on, on their blistered, frozen feet.

Like stray lambs, they sheltered against mountainsides under cover of great boulders, or of a dead, fallen tree, and warmed themselves at tremendous fires.

The little ones wailed and cried a thousand times a day; at the slightest provocation they sat down and refused to go any farther, but John drove them mercilessly onwards. Lizzy had long ceased to receive any of the precious milk. Indepentia looked half starved. She was so weak that her crying was hardly audible, and John sometimes doubted whether she was still breathing. He tried to warm her with his own breath, while listening for the beating of her heart. So soft it was – so feeble. . . .

The clothes they had been given at Fort Boisé – it seemed years ago now – hung round them in tatters, crumpled and weather-stained. They hardly spoke to each other; the children were afraid of John, even more afraid than they had been that time in the Snake Valley, where they had suffered from thirst, heat, flies, and mosquitoes. He was now even harder, even stricter, even more inexorable than he had been then.

One evening they were sitting in front of a big fire. Darkness fell early now; autumn was nearing its end. They stretched their purple, chapped, and swollen hands towards the warming glow. John sat morosely some distance apart from them, in utter wretchedness. Round about, wolves howled. Sometimes a pair of eyes would smoulder out of the darkness.

The children dropped off to sleep. They had had nothing to eat. John remained awake, keeping guard. He had Indepentia in his arms, with a wolf's skin round her.

He forced himself to stay awake by thinking of old times. The memory of those times was his only refuge. He no longer dared to dream of the future. He hardly dared to hope that they would ever reach the Columbia valley. They were certain to get snowed-up and starve, when the bitter winter began in earnest. He had no idea of the distance they still had to cover. The journey should not have taken so long.

He thought of old times. With an effort, he tried to picture Sunday morning on the farm near St Louis. Father with the Bible, Mother in her Sunday dress – Louise singing virtuously and out of tune, right above the others, he himself growling shyly. He was wearing a new suit, and Francis had been given his old one, together with a shining new leather belt by way of consolation. It smelt nice in the house, sweetish, fatty; Mother had been baking cakes. Lizzy was lying in the cradle; she crowed and beat the air with her little hands. She had fat little arms. Indepentia's arms were like twigs.

He pined for those old times; he pined so terribly for those old times. For steaming maize mush, for cake, for a fire on a hearthstone, for hot milk, for the deep bass voice of his father, for his mother's warm hand on the back of his neck – she always stroked the hairs on his neck the wrong way. For fat baby arms – oh, for fat baby arms. Suppose Indepentia . . .

He did not dare to follow his thought to the end. If she had to die, he would prefer that they all died. And all at the same time. Not one after the other. Please, please, oh please, not one after the other. Dear, good God, not one after the other.

Big, hot tears trickled down his cheeks. He opened a chink in the cloths, and let them drip on to Indepentia's little face. He could not have said why. It was all he had to give at that moment. And he was so lonely, and his heart was so full. 'Indepentia, Indepentia, darling, live, please, stay alive, won't you?'

A very faint sigh came from her tiny mouth; a little moan. He listened hungrily; he smiled in the darkness. He wrapped the wolf's fur close about her again. He rocked her in his arms. That kept one awake, too. He must not fall asleep. Wood had to be put on the fire. Those glowing wolves' eyes must not come any closer.

Next day, Cathie stubbornly refused to go any farther. With gritted teeth, John seized her by the arms, threw her across his knee, and spanked her until he could spank no more. Then he put the dazed child down on her feet again:

'Will you go on now?'

She nodded without speaking. She did not even cry. He would sooner have seen tears – then Cathie would have been more like herself. But she nodded dully, and began to walk.

He turned away with a jerk. He did not want to see the faces of the other children.

That same afternoon, Anna slipped and fell awkwardly on her side. Louise, who was walking next to her, was pinned beneath her. She shrieked. When the cow had scrambled to her feet again, Louise could not get up. John saw that she really could not get up. Her right leg lay twisted under her in a strange fashion. He wanted to straighten it. She screamed.

'It's broken, John.'

It *was* broken. Even a child could see that. He was

completely at a loss as to what to do. He stood looking at Louise, with his hands hanging helplessly at his sides. Louise moaned, and twisted and turned her head and shoulders from the pain. She bit her lips, hard.

They could go no farther. They made a fire. The place where they happened to be was fairly suitable.

The leg began to swell. John climbed to a small snowfield lying a short distance higher up the mountain, and there he made hard snowballs, which he threw down to Francis to catch. When there was a whole pile of them, John descended again. He pressed the snowballs against Louise's leg. He had once seen his father do that to the injured leg of a horse. The swelling had gone down then.

And that happened in this case, too. But it took a long time. Not that that mattered – they could not get any farther today, anyway. He did not dare think of the days that were to come.

They made their bivouac. When it was dark, Louise said to John, looking at him in the flickering light of the fire, with eyes big and black in her white, gaunt face:

'You go to sleep, John. I'll call you if anything happens, and if wood has to be put on the fire. I can't sleep, anyway.'

A minute later he was sleeping like a log.

It was Oscar who made the discovery, next morning.

For a long time, he had been running round restlessly sniffing, nosing at a scent which he would not leave but did not really dare to follow either. Francis went along with him. 'Not too far!' John called after them.

Oscar and Francis disappeared in the brown brushwood. Suddenly loud barking rang out, and Francis came running back. He beckoned with his arm, and shouted:

'John, John, your gun, quick!'

John ran. Francis went in front of him. They cleared a path for themselves between the swishing branches, to a place where Oscar's shrill barking was accompanied by a bloodcurdling growling.

In a den half dug in the ground, sheltered by a low cave in the wall of rock and well hidden behind dense undergrowth, an enormous, pallid old bear lay half on its back, half on its side. Its little eyes were concealed behind dirty tufts of reddish hair; its four paws, with their formidable talons, stuck forward. The animal growled terrifyingly, with open jaws.

When the children appeared behind the dog, the bear tried to get up. It raised itself a little; with lightning speed Oscar leapt forward and fixed his teeth in its bearded throat. The bear uttered a terrible roar, and rolled on to its feet with one last spasm of effort. Reeling, it stood on its shaggy, tufted hind legs.

John aimed, pulled the trigger – the gun misfired. But at the same moment the bear fell over on its back again, with Oscar on top of it.

John walked round a few paces, and tried to fire a second shot at its head. But the rifle misfired again.

The bear tried to get up once more. It could not. With a mighty swing of its left forepaw it swiped

Oscar away. The wolf dog yelped loudly, but sprang back on to the animal at once, and set his teeth in its throat for the second time.

The boys stood by, breathless. John did not even try to fire a third shot. The bear could do no more; it had been old and dying when Oscar found it – a solitary old male; and now the dog was putting a quicker end to its life, that was all. The blood flowed away from the wounds on its neck. It did not last long.

It was impossible to get Oscar to leave the dead bear. The boys walked slowly back to the girls.

'A bear – dead in his lair,' Francis got out.

The hollow faces showed a certain dull interest. Louise's only answer was a moan.

John sat down by the fire, and pointed to Francis's hunting knife. He wanted it. Francis gave it to him. John sharpened it against his own. When the two knives were as keen as razors, he went off again, back to the bear. Francis had to stay with the others and look after the fire.

John was busy all day. But when he had finished, the bear's hide had been scraped clean inside, and the girls sat with their legs buried in the old animal's thick winter coat. Big pieces of bear's meat were roasted above the fire; the fat dripped hissing into the flames; everyone could eat as much as he or she wanted. John had set traps and snares, using the bear's flesh as bait. He wanted to catch wolves, for the sake of their furs.

Anna had only yielded a few drops of milk that day. John melted snow, and blood which he pressed from the bear's meat, in a mug, and put it in the hot ash to get a bit warm. He thought the result might be something like beef tea. But when, finally, he managed, with infinite patience, to pour it all drop by drop into Indepentia's little mouth, she vomited more up than she had taken in. Then she turned up her eyes and lay more dead than alive in his arms. Desperately he looked at Louise, but her leg was hurting her too much; she lay livid, moaning, with closed eyes.

Francis seized the mug, walked up to the cow with it, and pulled gently but insistently at the wretched animal's limp udder. Anna turned her bony, emaciated head, and looked at him with big faithful eyes: pull, lad, pull! I'll give what I have. . . . Four, five, six large drops came out. And that was all.

'We'll stay here,' John decided. 'We'll move to the bear's den, it's big enough for all of us to lie in it. I'll cut the brushwood away from in front, so that we can have a fire. We'll be warm and sheltered there. We'll stay there until the bear's meat's gone, we'll eat as much as we can every day. Higher up there's enough snow for water, and perhaps Louise will have less pain if she can lie down for a few days. I'll see to it that we get wolf's skins. Francis will see to wood, and to the fire; and the others can go out and look for food for Anna, from morning till night.'

That was their only chance. The cow *had* to be kept on her feet. She had to start giving a bit of milk again, and she had to be able to carry Louise on her back – otherwise, how would they ever be able to get on?

The bear's lair stank. A pungent, rancid odour stung their nostrils. But they had the feeling that they were moving into a house. A deliciously warm, safe house, with a roof and a floor and a fire in an open hearth. Cathie, who had eaten until she was round and satisfied, began to perk up again.

'Oooh, what a smell! But it's nice and warm!' She nestled down cosily against the wall. 'Even nicer than the pigsty at home. Jiminy, what skinny pigs we all are!'

'*You've* gorged so much, you're quite fat enough for the butcher. It'll soon be Christmas,' said Francis.

'Don't say such idiotic things,' Cathie suddenly burst out, with a jerk of her shoulders and with tears in her eyes. 'How on earth can you talk about Christmas *here*?'

'At Christmas we shall be at Dr Whitman's mission station,' John said slowly. 'Then we shall have goose with roasted apples, and cake and . . .' They listened in amazement to this cheerful note from John's lips.

'. . . and nuts, and oranges,' Cathie added, suddenly feeling that she wanted to hear about Christmas after all. 'And pancakes with bramble jelly.'

'And at Christmas, we'll dance,' Matilda chimed in, in a dreamy tone, with her eyes fixed on the fire.

. . . Or we shall be lying under the snow, thought John; but the children don't need to know that.

He listened thankfully to Francis and Cathie bickering. Was it to be red or black bramble jelly? Louise lay without speaking, but her eyes were open, and she was the only one who saw John smile.

Suddenly she began to understand him a little.

They stayed in the bear's den for six days. By then, the meat was gone. And John dared not stop any longer. The mountain passes were already deep under snow.

Another six arduous days' marches followed.

On the second day, they had already forgotten what it felt like to have a full stomach. On the third day they were dragging themselves along on trembling legs. On the fourth day Cathie had to have another thrashing. On the fifth day Louise slid unconscious off Anna's knobbly back, and had to be tied on again with thongs of wolf's skin. Indepentia had ceased to give any sign of life. Nevertheless, John repeatedly managed to work a few drops of milk between her tiny, closed lips.

In three days they had climbed a mountain ridge. In two days they had descended it on the other side. Yesterday they had stood at the foot of the following ridge, and John had pointed to its snow-crowned top and said: 'Perhaps this is the last.' No one believed any longer that there was a last.

Now they were plodding on through the deep snow. It really looked as if they would never reach that ridge. John was crueller and harsher than ever; he was at his wit's end, and he constantly had to conceal his despair. Their only chance of salvation lay in his remaining mercilessly severe.

He walked on in front. He had to lift his feet as if heavy, dead weights hung on them. He made a path for the others. Under the snow the rocky ground was sharp and rough, but even the snow pierced his sore, cut, badly swaddled feet as with a thousand needles. His heart thumped against his ribs. Indepentia, who weighed nothing, was a lead-like burden in his aching arms.

Doggedly pushing on, he came nearer and nearer to the top. Once he was there, he would lay Indepentia down and go back and fetch the others. He could already hear them crying. Now and again, he caught the voice of Francis from below, urging the girls on, and talking to Anna. Louise was a brick. Ever since they had left the bear's den, she had not made a sound of complaint. Her broken leg dangled limply down Anna's lean flank.

He had reached the top. He made his last steps slowly, very slowly. He looked down over the other side. He saw . . .

That . . . that was impossible! How could it be, so – so suddenly? It was such a wonderful sight, what he saw there. So splendid, so unbelievable, so . . . it must be an optical illusion, he thought. He shook his head and shut his eyes. Then he opened them again. He looked at Indepentia, he looked down . . . it was *not* an optical illusion, it was what he had been hungering for all those weeks, and now that it was there he could not believe it.

Far below him, far below this last chain of the Blue Mountains, lay a wide, long, green valley, with trees and shrubs still clad in their autumn yellow. There were the small square shapes of a few log cabins, a thin plume of smoke rose from a chimney – it was the mission station of Dr Marcus Whitman. It was Oregon; it must be the Columbia valley. Down there he saw a winding, silver ribbon with edges of luxuriant green.

Great Father in Heaven, they were there!

He did not look round at the others. He did not beckon and he did not wave; he did not shout. He stood motionless, gazing down, and let them come.

12

Now their bleeding feet had climbed the last mountain ridge; now they were standing on the crest of the whole massif, staring down into that broad green valley in the west. Behind them stretched a prehistoric landscape – a labyrinth of mountains cut by deep canyons, a hard, savage world in black and white. Like patient snails they had found their way, creeping up and creeping down, a tiny caravan of insignificant dwarfs in the land of the giants.

Beneath them, at the foot of the long, long last slope, stretched the green valley, warm in its autumn colours.

Yonder, in the depths, wound the Columbia River.

Farther off, and round about, extending far into the remote distance, where the whole world turned blue, the majestic hill country of Oregon lay spread before them in a tremendous panorama.

There was the land where all promises and dreams would come true.

The children stared down. They shivered. John did not allow them much time to rest. With groping steps, he began the long descent. Slowly they came behind him, down – down – down. Oscar ran on in front.

John walked as if in a dream.

His legs, swathed in pieces of wolf's hide, seemed totally numb. Nevertheless, they continued to carry him. He stared into the depths. A strip of leather kept his long hair out of his eyes. On his back he was carrying little Lizzy, in his arms the bundle of fur containing Indepentia, who had not made a single movement, not given a sign of life, for many hours now, and perhaps was dead. . . .

Behind John waddled the cow.

She groaned; descending was much more difficult for her than climbing, and her worn hooves were split down to the quick.

On the open, inflamed, dirty galls on her skinny back, Louise and Matilda sagged like limp dolls, wrapped in rags and wolf skins. It was as if there was no light left in their eyes, no blood left in their cheeks, no strength, no sap, left in their whole bodies. Their hair hung long and tangled round their heads.

Francis and Cathie were walking – they hobbled, they were exhausted with hunger and fatigue, their faces were grey, gaunt, and dull; Francis urged Cathie onwards in a weak, husky voice, which she did not hear.

They crept down the slope, they stumbled, fell, scrambled to their feet again, dragged themselves on, coughing, panting. Francis's breath wheezed. Even now, John still had the greatest difficulty in keeping them moving – still, with the end in sight, they would sooner have laid down and died where they were; still he had to pause and wait, chivvy them, be rough and hard. . . .

And at last, at last, in a silence that was more heartrending than the loudest weeping, they stood in that valley of the blest, before the door of Dr Whitman's log house.

John pushed the door open with his knee.

A young woman with a pale, weary face, came forward.

John looked at her.

She uttered an unintelligible cry when she saw the group of little ghosts – the wasted children's faces, the cow which was no more than a caricature of a cow, and yet was so touching with its big, lean head.

The children remained silent, they could not say a word. John made a feeble movement with his arms. Narcissa Whitman put out her hands and took the little bundle from him. She motioned to him to follow her.

Cathie tripped over the doorstep. She remained lying there until Francis helped her up. John helped Matilda to slide down from the cow, and set her on her feet. She tottered into the house. He helped Louise off too, but she fell moaning to the ground, and could not get up. He could not help her. He went inside.

They came into a big kitchen. There was an enormous brick stove in it, and the room smelt of savoury meat cooked with salt.

A man was standing there. He was dressed like a trapper and wearing a woollen cap. His face was forceful and bearded, his eyes stared incredulously out from under bristly eyebrows. He said not a word; his gaze travelled from one to the other, dwelt a second or two longer on John, and then turned to Narcissa, his wife. His eyes narrowed to slits. She had laid the baby on the table; hungrily, she tore open the fur and the rags. Their own only child, a little girl, had been drowned in the river two years ago. But when she saw what was lying under those rags stiff with dirt, she backed away. With wide, staring eyes, she looked at Indepentia. Dr Whitman followed her gaze. A breathless silence hung in the kitchen.

John's suspense was unbearable. His eyes begged for an answer to his unspoken question.

'Perhaps there's still some life left in it,' was all Marcus Whitman could say.

Narcissa Whitman took the tiny skeleton into the bedroom with her. Her husband made to take the other children to a washroom in one of the outbuildings of the mission post. But John refused. He jerked his head in the direction of the door through which Mrs Whitman had disappeared.

'Lad, lad, you can't do anything to help there, anyway,' said Dr Whitman.

John still said not a word. He remained stubbornly standing where he was, looking at the door.

But then he suddenly remembered: Louise! Louise is still lying outside!

He motioned to the doctor. Whitman followed the strange boy out of the house. He lifted the girl, who lay unconscious on the ground, up in his arms. The child did not weigh much more than that tiny baby could have weighed. Her leg looked nasty; it was fractured in two places, inflamed and swollen. Louise's head dangled limply back like a bird's.

Dr Whitman spread a blanket out on the floor in the kitchen and put her down on it. He poured drops of milk, one by one, between her half-open lips. When she came to, he laid another blanket over her, and let her lie there while he went back to the others.

John had vanished.

As if drawn by a magnet, he had walked through the doorway through which Indepentia had been carried. He came into a sitting-room with a table and chairs and a ticking grandfather clock, a mirror, and books; another door stood open and, as if in a dream, he walked through into a bedroom.

Narcissa Whitman was bathing Indepentia in warm water.

John stood behind them. He saw the tiny frame, nothing but sticks of bones and skin, being rubbed and massaged with warm oil, by gentle hands – he saw her being wrapped in clean woollen cloths. But she still gave not a single sign of life. Narcissa Whitman held a mirror in front of her mouth. Did the glass become misty or not? She couldn't be sure; she rubbed the mirror clean on her sleeve, tried again, was still not sure.

Carefully, she pressed a few drops of warm milk and water between the baby's purple lips. Moments of unbearable suspense followed. John held his breath. He reeled on his feet. He would have liked to *look* life into the child.

At last, its tiny throat made a movement as if it was swallowing, and a sound came out of it, even fainter than the cheeping of a little bird.

When John heard that, he fell to the ground, threw his arms round Narcissa Whitman's knees, and burst out sobbing. His shoulders shook, his arms dropped to her feet, he collapsed on the floor and wept and laughed at the same time.

Mrs Whitman let him cry it out. She stroked his hair, deeply moved.

Finally, John got up. He did not look at her. Without saying a word he stumbled from the room.

Meanwhile, Dr Whitman had been busy with the others. He had made them presentable and human again, washed them, cut their hair, and given them clothes. Now they were sitting at table in the kitchen, gorging like wolves.

The whole night through, Narcissa Whitman sat up with the child in her lap. Her back and shoulders ached, her eyes smarted, but she concentrated all her strength on her desire to keep the baby alive.

John, washed and tidied up, in clean clothes, was sleeping on a fur at her feet. Dr Whitman was lying on a camp bed beside her. He lay with his hands folded behind his head, and with open eyes. He did not need to look at John to be constantly aware of the boy's presence. There was something about that lad, something emanated from him – a strange power, a strength of will such as Marcus Whitman had never yet encountered.

At first, John Sager had exacted merely cold admiration from him. The boy had achieved something, and caused something to be achieved, which was unbelievable. He must necessarily be a born tyrant and bully. Yes . . . those had been the doctor's first feelings. But now?

Marcus Whitman smiled in the darkness. Before they went to bed, something had happened. He could still feel that shaking, thin body against his, that boy's head on his shoulder. . . .

'Take the load off me,' John had sobbed. 'I can't go on, I can't. They don't love me any more, they couldn't understand, and I love *them* so much. . . . I had to be so strict and horrid to them, I've beaten them, I've dragged them along . . . and now we've got here, and they don't love me any more! Please, please, won't you be our father, *I* can't go on! Won't you, please?'

Dr Whitman had patted him on the back. He had spoken soothing words to him.

But that had not been any use. John had repeated his question, urgently, imploringly, with burning eyes.

'Won't you be our father? I want to . . . play with them again.' That last had been spoken very softly. Like an admission of guilt.

It had moved Dr Whitman more than anything else. The boy had done something superhuman – hardly any grown man could have done it, even. But he had suffered much under his far too heavy task and responsibility, and now he wanted to play again . . . to play with his sisters and his brother and the baby.

. . . Oh, what was the name of that child, now? Indepentia – Independence! You didn't know whether to laugh or cry about it!

It was no trifle, to take seven children into his household – seven more mouths to feed. Seven children, a wolf dog, and a cow; and *what* a cow! The most extraordinary thing in the way of cows which he had ever come across in his life. The animal did not feel at all at home in the warm shelter of the stall, along with the other cows and without the children. But he could hardly have invited Anna to take her place at table!

If his wife had not been so wretched, and almost at the end of her tether, then . . . well, there was no telling what he might have decided. But that solitary life there, with nothing about her except, now and again, hypocritical Indian faces, was killing her. And yet there *was* a future in this country. Nevertheless, it would become populated; nevertheless, here, in the distant future, farms and villages and perhaps even towns would arise. And to achieve that, men and women were needed who were made of the same stuff as the Sager children.

He put out his hand and touched his wife's knee.

'I believe she'll make it,' Narcissa whispered. 'She's breathing regularly now.'

'It's a miracle,' the doctor-missionary whispered back. 'It's all a miracle. Is it meant to be a sign to us, Narcissa?'

'Oh, Marcus,' came his wife's gentle voice, with a sigh. 'Oh, Marcus, do you think you could possibly let them all stay here?'

A deep, soft laugh sounded in his throat. He growled something which Narcissa did not hear; but then she felt his warm hand squeeze her knee, and that told her what she wanted to know.

The following morning, as they sat at breakfast in the

big kitchen, Dr Whitman told the children of his decision, in words that were brief and to the point:

'From now on, this is your home. And John's relieved of his job of father. Look upon me as your father, and my wife as your mother. May your heroic journey be the beginning of a highly promising future as American citizens. God bless our covenant. Amen.'

On the third Sunday after they arrived, Indepentia was christened. With a beaming face, John held her for baptism. Fifty or so Indian men, women and children who had been converted to Christianity attended the simple service.

When John left the log cabin which did duty as a church, carrying the child in his arms, he looked up at once at the snow-crowned peaks of the Blue Mountains. Then he bent his face right over Indepentia and whispered:

'Little bag of bones, how on earth did you get here? I can't for the life of me understand!'

But behind him, Cathie's voice chimed boastfully:

'Look, that was the slope we slid down.' And, a moment or two later, more to herself and with a sigh of relief: 'Uhuh, at last that child's been baptised!'